Body Market

Andrew Leatham

This edition published in 2017 by Endeavour Press Ltd.

CHAPTER 1

Afterwards, none of those who had heard the row in the run-down apartment block — a rotting tooth in a jawbone of identical buildings on the outskirts of Rotterdam — would agree on how long it had lasted. Some would say it went on for almost an hour. Some would say it went on for longer, while others would claim it was over in minutes. All of them would agree that the shouting and screaming was mainly in English with a smattering of another language that could have been Arabic. And all of them would agree that even though they could not make out exactly what was being yelled, it was obvious that a young woman was deeply distressed and in fear of the two male voices with whom she was arguing.

Yet not one of them lifted a finger to help; not one of them dared knock on the door and not one of them picked up the phone to call the police.

***

Mia was 23 years-old, slimly built and beautiful in the way that is unique to Arab women. Her milky coffee coloured skin was flawless; her cheekbones high; her big, almond-shaped eyes were deep brown, so brown that at first glance they looked black, highlighted by perfectly arched dark eye-brows; her lips full and wide. Lustrous auburn hair cascaded over her shoulders.

Before the civil war began, she had been a medical student in Damascus but as conditions deteriorated, she and her father — the only living relative she had — decided to flee. But the onslaught by rebel forces and the fury of the retaliation by Government troops constantly pinned them down, restricting their movements, forcing them from one shared house to another until, dejected, despondent and downcast, they submitted to the final indignity and found themselves living in a make-shift tent in a squalid, overcrowded refugee camp.

It was in the camp — living, as Mia wrote in her diary, 'like rats on a city dump' — that her father met a man who offered a sliver of hope. The man said he knew someone who could get them out of Syria and to a new life in Europe, if they had the money. It would cost, he said,

$15,000. Each. They would be given new identities and all the relevant permits that would allow them to live freely in Britain. Mia's father didn't think to query why, as legitimate refugees, they would need false identities. All he cared about was getting his beautiful, intelligent daughter to somewhere where should could continue her studies and one day achieve her dream of becoming a surgeon.

As a structural engineer in Damascus, he had lived a fairly comfortable life; never short of money, nice house, nice car, nice family. But now all that he owned was carried on his back. And he knew it wasn't enough for both of them to escape the hell which they were currently living in. His 'contact,' however, was willing to do a deal and eventually, he handed over all of his late wife's jewellery, including several gold bracelets, necklaces and diamond rings to give his precious Mia the chance of a new life.

Their parting was heart-breaking for both of them. Mia promised to write. Her father promised they would be together again soon. Both of them knew they were lies. The chances of them ever being together again were, at best, remote and in reality, unattainable. As they parted, her father pressed a small leather bag into Mia's hand. 'Just in case you need it,' he whispered. 'Don't let anyone know you have it. Hide it somewhere it will never be found.'

Inside the bag was an uncut diamond, about the size of a pea, which even in its raw state would have been worth more than enough money to allow him to join his daughter. It was, he maintained, his 'insurance policy' but against what he never specified. Today, all that mattered was that his daughter had at least something to fall back on should she need it when she reached her new home.

Three weeks and several hundred uncomfortable, cramped and humiliating miles later, Mia found herself in Rotterdam, sleeping in a damp, smelly bunk bed in a run-down flat with several other girls, each and every one of them refugees from the Middle East or Africa, seeking a new life. Their saviour was an Englishman in his late 30s, who had promised each of them jobs, security and more money than they could dream of when he finally got them to England.

Mike Pilling carried the look of someone constantly angry. His thin lips were twisted in a permanent snarl; his small, deeply set, piggy eyes gave him the appearance of a living skull. The skin of his face was pock-marked by a childhood illness and wrinkled like a prune, a condition made worse by his addiction to cigarettes and liberal use of recreational drugs. Down each side of his face a narrow line of unshaven stubble met on his chin, making his greasy brown hair look like it was tied on.

But all that the girls saw was salvation.

On her fourth morning in the flat, Mia awoke to find herself alone. The other girls had gone, leaving behind no sign that they had ever been there. She checked every room in the apartment. There was no one. She had no idea where she was; apart from the uncut diamond she had no means of support and absolutely no idea what to do next. She thought she should eat and found a box of cereal in a kitchen cupboard. She filled a bowl and opened the fridge for milk but without even touching it, she could see that it had turned sour. Distraught, she went back to her bunk and cried herself to sleep.

She was awakened by the sound of voices, two English male voices, from the living room next door. She crept out of bed and tip-toed to the door.

'What you going to do with this one then?' asked a voice she didn't recognise.

'I've got plans for her,' replied Mike Pilling. 'Have you had a close look? We can make a fortune out of her, she's something special. First job is to get her to London. Then we train her up on the pole and put her on in an up-market club. It won't be long before the punters are gagging for it. I reckon we could easily charge a grand a night for her; even more when she gets experience.'

'You not going to start her off in one of the ordinary places?' asked the voice. 'So she can learn the ropes.'

'What and pick up all the filthy habits those other slags have got? No chance mate. This one's pure class. She's got to be treated right. High-end punters only.'

Outside the door the truth of her situation suddenly dropped on Mia like a plane crash. Far from being given a new identity and being able to finish her training as a doctor, she was to be forced into prostitution; to become a plaything for fat, greasy men; to have her body perpetually used and abused. Suddenly, she yearned to be back in the refugee camp; back with her father; to feel the comfort of his embrace.

Without really considering the consequences, she slammed through the door into the living room where she found Pilling and another man drinking whisky. 'No,' she screamed. 'I won't do it. I won't.'

'Ah, here she is,' said Pilling, looking admiringly at the girl who still managed to be beautiful without make-up and dressed in a T-shirt and baggy track-suit bottoms. 'Won't do what princess? What are you talking about?'

'I know what you have planned and I'm not doing it. I won't be a whore,' screamed Mia. 'I'm going to be a doctor. You promised my father. He paid you. He paid you a lot of money. Everything he had. You can't do this...'

Pilling took a swig of his scotch. 'Thing is sweetheart, as far as I'm concerned, your dad and me did a deal. He sold you to me. Your mine now and that means I can do what the fuck I like with you. Got it?'

Tears flowed freely down Mia's perfect cheeks. 'No, he didn't sell me,' she shouted. 'He paid you to take me to England; to safety; away from the fighting. You have to stick to your side of the bargain. You have to keep your promise.'

'Listen princess, I don't have to do anything I don't want to,' shouted Pilling. 'If your old man was stupid enough to believe anything that may or may not have been said during the course of our negotiations, that's his problem. Understand? Now, if I want you to make me a fucking fortune on your fucking back, that's exactly what you will fucking do. Right?'

Mia let out an ear-piercing scream, turned on her heels and fled back to her bunk.

Pilling sighed. 'Georgie, go and bring her back,' he said to his companion. 'But don't damage her. I don't want her knocked about.'

George Curtis stood a little under six feet tall but his build was such that he gave the impression of being square. His large head, covered in closely-cropped blonde hair, seemed to blend into his body without the benefit of a neck. His hands were the size of spades and his thighs were as thick as most men's waists. 'Pleasure Mike,' was all he said.

From the bedroom next door came screams and shouts and a stream of Arabic swear words, then the sound of furniture being knocked over, followed by even more screaming, shouting and swearing. Eventually Curtis reappeared in the living room with Mia over his shoulder in a fireman's lift. His right arm was through her legs and he gripped both her wrists in his right hand. Her track suit bottoms had slipped down, exposing her backside.

'Lovely George, lovely,' said Pilling peering over the rim of his glass. 'Chuck her on the sofa and get her kit off. Let's have a look at what we've really got.'

Mia fought with every ounce of strength she possessed but it was fruitless. In less than a minute, the flimsy garments had been torn off and she lay naked, trying as best she could to cover her body; to hide it from the gaze of these westerners.

'Now that's really, really nice,' said Pilling as Curtis dragged the sobbing girl to her feet and pinned her arms behind her. 'Really nice. I think this one's going to be a very good investment George. Probably the best we've ever had.'

'Bastard. Lying, cheating dirty bastard,' screamed Mia. 'You can't make me. I won't. Do what you want but I won't.'

A smile played across Pilling's lips. 'I think you'll find we can be very persuasive,' he said. 'By the time we've finished with you, you'll be begging to fuck some old bastard, just for a rest. Tell you what, while we're here, I think I might have a go myself. Hold her down George.'

His hand moved to his belt buckle as he took a pace towards the terrified girl.

'No. Please. No. Don't. I'm a virgin,' she sobbed, as if the revelation might somehow save her. 'I'm a virgin. Please...'

Miraculously, Pilling stopped. His piggy eyes lit up. 'A virgin eh?' he said. 'Well we'll check that out when we get to England. If you're telling the truth, there are men out there who would pay handsomely for the privilege. But God help you if you're lying...'

'I'm not, I'm not,' Mia mumbled through her tears as she fell to her knees, her arms encircling her breasts, hiding them from view.

As she knelt, quaking in fear, Pilling produced a chain-store carrier bag from behind a chair and threw it front of her. 'Here, put this lot on,' he ordered. 'You'll be leaving tonight and I want you to look the part — smart, modern but just another passenger. And no make-up. I don't want you attracting unnecessary attention.

'George, you and her and the car are booked on the eight o'clock ferry to Hull. I've booked you a cabin. Make sure she stays in it. I don't want her talking to anybody. Understand?'

***

The ferry had been at sea for two hours and was well out into the North Sea en route for Hull. The cabin that Pilling had paid for was basic, deep down in the middle of the ship with no natural light and no natural ventilation. But at least it had a shower and a toilet so Curtis was secure in the knowledge that Mia had no reason to leave and therefore had no opportunity to blurt out her plight to a fellow passenger or a member of the crew.

'Listen, bitch,' Curtis snarled at Mia. 'He might think the sun shines out of your arse but to me you're just another whore. I'm going for a drink. Don't you fucking dare leave this cabin. I'll know if you do and you won't like the result. Just stay put. OK?'

Mia, sitting on the top bunk with her knees under her chin, could only nod in fear.

She waited for half an hour before opening the cabin door and venturing outside. Still dressed in the clothes she had boarded in — jeans, heavy jumper, quilted body-warmer and a beanie hat — she had no notion of whereabouts in the ship she was. Then she spotted a sign that indicated: 'Lifeboat Deck This Way.' She followed the signs up several flights of stairs, each one wider than the one before until she found herself staring out through an armoured glass door into the darkness beyond.

The door opened to her touch and she stepped out onto the port side lifeboat deck, a little less than half way down the length of the ship. She was surprised by how cold it was and how much the wind whistled over the deck. To her right and above her she could see the dim lights from the bridge but there was not another living soul around. Using the davits to which the lifeboats were secured as a handhold, Mia climbed onto the ship's rail and stared down into the blackness beneath her.

She stayed there, silent and still, watching the waves below. Images raced through her brain: images of her mother; of her father; of the friends she'd had as a child; of the friends she'd made at university and of the destruction of Damascus. Finally, the decision was made...

Her cry of 'Baba. As tagh firullah' — *Father. I seek forgiveness from Allah* — was lost on the wind as she gave herself, unseen and unheard, to the cold, heartless embrace of the North Sea.

The suction generated by the ship's forward movement dragged her body, already broken by the uncontrolled fall of nearly a hundred feet, under the hull. Seconds later the twin counter-rotating propellers, each weighing 15 tonnes and turning at 500 revolutions a minute, churned her fragile remains into mincemeat.

As the ship sailed on, a red cloud of human flesh and shards of bone descended gently to the sea floor, more than 300 feet below, to become fodder for fish, crabs and lobsters.

Amongst the falling cloud of gore was a small leather bag.

***

Curtis went into a panic when he finally returned from the bar and found her gone. The impact rapidly countered the affects of the five pints of strong lager and two whiskies he had drunk. His first thoughts were that she had to be on the ship somewhere; that she was simply hiding. But where? He had no idea. He had no option: he had to report her missing.

Taking her new, false, Italian passport, which gave her name as Francesca Tommasi, aged 23, he went to find the purser's office, where he blurted out his story to a female officer. He told her he had gone for a drink and found his girlfriend missing when he returned to their cabin. He'd searched everywhere but couldn't find her and he was worried.

The woman listened patiently and without outward signs of panic, as if this was an everyday occurrence. She took the passport, went into a small back office and rang the bridge to report a missing passenger. 'Shit, shit, shit,' was the captain's immediate response, closely followed by instructions to broadcast an appeal for the woman over the ship's Tannoy and to organise a stem-to-stern search of every nook and cranny on the vessel. Then he ordered the ship to heave-to and radioed the Humber Coastguard on VHF Channel 16 to inform them of the situation and what was being done. When he'd done that, he switched the Coastguard to the private communications channel and gave them what details he had of the missing passenger.

By the time the captain appeared at the purser's office, Curtis was doing a good job of being upset and devastated at the apparent loss of his girlfriend. He repeated his story and kept saying: 'I just want her back.' He denied vehemently that they'd had a row. He'd gone to the bar alone because she wanted to sleep. The bar steward confirmed he had been alone and had spoken to no one except the staff.

It took just over an hour to complete the sweep of the ship but, as Curtis was praying, not a sign of Mia/Francesca was found, other than the few clothes she had left behind in the cabin. There were no indications of a struggle anywhere on board. And there had been no response to the repeated Tannoy call for passenger Francesca Tomassi to report to the Purser's Office. The Captain again radioed Humber Coastguard and told them there was no sign of the missing passenger on board his vessel and he was therefore declaring a Man Over Board, even though he had no clue as to precisely where and when she last seen.

The Coastguard Maritime Rescue Co-Ordination Centre in Bridlington issued an immediate All Ships alert about the missing girl, giving the position she had been lost as somewhere between two hours out of Rotterdam and the ferry's position when the Captain reported her missing. Every skipper of every vessel that heard the call had the same thought: it was too late. Wherever she had gone overboard, she would be dead by now.

When the ferry arrived in Hull, police were waiting to interview witnesses and found exactly none. Being the last person to see her alive, Curtis was taken in for questioning and put on a performance that amazed even him. He played the heartbroken boyfriend, even managing tears as he told his interviewers that he had first met Francesca working in a refugee camp in Syria when he was a driver with an aid convoy. They had fallen in love but as the violence increased they both became frightened for their lives and decided to run. At the first airport they came to, the first plane out was heading for Holland. They had been living in Rotterdam for several weeks, earning enough money to buy an old car and tickets for the ferry to England and the new life they had planned there.

It didn't take long for police to establish that George Curtis was indeed a long-distance lorry driver, employed, as he had claimed, by Pilling Transport of Colchester. His passport showed that he had also driven a vehicle carrying refugee aid to Syria, although he appeared to have crossed the border into that country illegally — not an offence to cause the British police any concern. His story seemed to check out on every level.

They also interviewed the ferry Captain and the Office of the Watch. But 48 hours after the ship had docked, the file was already gathering dust.

CHAPTER 2

Two thousand miles away Ray Wilson was in paradise.

Big, fat grapes, their skins almost black, hung down in giant bunches from a canopy of green that provided the bar with a shield against the blistering heat of the afternoon sun. Behind his head a gleaming white marble plaque carried the date 1871 and a Greek cross — the *crux immissaa quadrata* — with its distinctive four equal-length arms. Exactly what the stone signified he had no idea but, like a million tourists before him, he assumed it marked the year of the building's birth.

Even if he had been sufficiently interested, there was no one around he could ask. Not that the bar was empty. He was sharing the outdoor space with a dozen or so elderly Greek men, some sporting luxuriant moustaches, who were talking animatedly, arguing, smoking and drinking, mostly iced coffee through straws, some of them with ouzo chasers. The problem was none of them spoke English and his Greek was limited to a handful of words that allowed him to say 'Hello,' 'Please' and 'Thank You.' Hardly the basis for an intelligent conversation on the island's history.

In front of him, a steep pine-covered valley dropped 2,000 feet to a golden beach three miles away and the rippling calm of the Aegean Sea, glistening in the harsh sunlight like deep blue satin. The main road that ran around the island curved past the bar, a tarmac boomerang carelessly dropped on the hillside, climbing fiercely out of the valley in a steep slope that had proved to many a mountain biker where the edge of fitness lay. To his English mind, calling it a road was something of an exaggeration — it was more of a country lane, in places barely wide enough for two vehicles to pass, not that there was much traffic beyond the hourly local bus and a few hire cars driven by petrified holidaymakers.

Ray sat alone, sipping an ice-cold Mythos beer, listening to the chatter of the locals yet not understanding a word of it, his mind empty of all that had gone before. He tried to remember the last time he had a proper holiday but it was so long ago, his recall was blurred. It was somewhere on the Costa Brava. Or was it Majorca? All he knew for certain was that he was a much younger man and life had been much simpler. But the last job, hunting the sadistic killer of two young girls, had left Detective Chief Inspector Ray Wilson of the West Yorkshire Police Major Incident Unit, exhausted physically and emotionally and desperately in need of a break.

His first thought had been to indulge his passion and charter a yacht to sail the beautiful Dalmation coast. But he quickly realised that the charter companies were set up to deal with families and big parties, not middle-aged single men. A couple of operators offered him the chance to share a charter with other singles, but the prospect of being cooped up in a space 45 feet by 12 feet with a bunch of complete strangers appalled him. He did eventually find a small local company that was willing to charter him a boat but the price they quoted made it obvious they had no real desire for his business.

He was beginning to despair until one of his team mentioned the Greek island of Thassos. Unspoilt by tourism, mountainous, pine covered and quiet it seemed to offer everything he was looking for and so, a week later, he found himself on board a holiday company's jet, heading for two weeks of peace and solitude.

The bar in which he was currently drinking — it didn't appear to have a name; its very anonymity making it even more attractive — was everything he had anticipated a local Greek bar being. He had been there for close on two hours, had lost count of the number of beers he had swallowed and hadn't yet parted with a cent. He was sure, though, that the dark-haired girl who appeared to be the only staff the bar had, would know exactly. She flitted between the tables, collecting empties, replacing them with fresh drinks and dispensing free bowls of snacks, sometimes delicious, moist pistachio nuts, sometimes small cheesy biscuits, sometimes crisps. And every time his drink got to within an inch of the bottom, she would ask him: 'Another beer?' Ray felt slightly embarrassed at the fact that this girl's English was far superior than his own meagre grasp of her native tongue, but managed to respond with: 'Nai parakelo,' which even though it sounded negative, meant 'Yes please.'

He was so comfortable, so relaxed and so happy but part of him was saying he couldn't stay there forever, that soon he would have to stir himself. He had already promised himself there would just be one more.

And then that the next one would be the ABL — Absolute Bloody Last. But that was two bottles back and he had just ordered another.

Just as the girl put the bottle down in front of him, he felt the mobile phone in his pocket vibrate and emit a sound that signalled the arrival of a text message. He ignored it. He was on holiday; he wasn't a slave to technology. Whatever it was, it could wait. He took a long draught of beer and watched a yacht way out on the horizon, making steady progress to the North, igniting a brief spark of envy. The beer and the afternoon sun combined to make him feel sleepy so, half way down the glass, curiosity and the urge to stay awake got the better of him and he opened the text.

It said: 'Ring me urgently. Greenwood.' The text gave an unlisted number that Ray recognised. It was a direct-line to Colin Greenwood that by-passed his secretary. And Colin Greenwood was the Chief Constable of West Yorkshire Police. His boss.

Ray stared at the message as if puzzling out what it meant; what was so important that the Chief Constable would contact him personally? While he was on holiday. A host of ideas tumbled through his brain, not one of them viable. He could think of no valid reason why the Chief would send him a text message from 2,000 miles away. So he did something that once would have been unthinkable.

He put the phone back in his pocket and ordered another beer.

As the afternoon sun gradually sank behind the mountains and shadows became longer and softer, Ray finally decided it was time to go. He paid his bill, gave the girl an over-generous 10 Euro tip and asked if she would get him a taxi. She smiled, turned to a man sitting at another table and said something very quickly in Greek. The man stood and walked off. Less than a minute later he reappeared behind the wheel of a silver Mercedes saloon and beckoned Ray to get in.

As the car pulled up outside the apartment block where Ray was staying, his mobile signalled the arrival of another text. He had no need to look what it said, nor who it was from.

**

The following morning, hung-over and contrite, Ray took advantage of the two hour time difference between Greece and West Yorkshire to try to swallow some blotting paper before making the call that, deep down, he knew he should have made the previous day. He managed a bowl of yoghurt and grapes, drizzled in the local Thassian delicacy, pine honey, followed by a couple of bites from yesterday's loaf that was already on the verge of staleness. Half a pint of orange juice lubricated the way down to his tumbling stomach. But all he really wanted to do was lie in the sun and feel sorry for himself.

Eventually, he couldn't put it off any longer so with trepidation in his heart, he dialled the number on the text message. It rang just twice before an unhurried voice answered simply: 'Greenwood.'

'Good morning sir, it's DCI Wilson. I've got a message to call you,' ventured Ray.

'Wilson. Where the bloody hell have you been? I've been trying to contact you for days.'

Actually, no you haven't. You sent me a couple of text messages yesterday. Not what you'd call desperation, thought Ray, but deference to rank and the need for diplomacy meant he kept his counsel.

'Sorry sir. I'm on holiday in Greece and the mobile reception's a bit dodgy. I only received your texts this morning. I rang as soon as possible.' It was the default excuse for all mobile callers, as he well knew, but in his condition it was the best he could manage.

'The thing is, something's cropped up and we need you back here immediately,' said Greenwood, his accent more estuary English than his native Geordie, altered — imperceptibly to him — by his years working his way through the ranks that had taken him to most corners of the country. 'For reasons I'm sure you will understand I can't tell you any more at this moment. We just need to get you back to the UK ASAP.'

'I understand sir,' said Ray. 'But the problem is that the airport I flew into only deals with holiday flights. I can't get out until my flight leaves next Wednesday.'

'We've already thought of that Wilson. How quickly can you get on a ferry to Kavalla?'

'I'd need to check the exact times but I think they run pretty regularly at this time of year.'

'Good. Ring me when you can confirm a time you will be in Kavalla. Someone will pick you up and take you to the airport at Thessalonika.' Without further explanation or pleasantries, Greenwood hung up, leaving Ray staring at his mobile, overwhelmed by the feeling that he'd just been mugged.

***

Twenty four hours later he was standing on the quayside in Kavalla, his leather and canvas bag at his feet, feeling somewhat lost, when a young man approached him. The immaculately pressed lightweight grey suit, stiff-collared white shirt, Grenadier Guards tie, all topped off by a Panama hat, instantly marked him out as a Brit — and not one on holiday.

'Mr Wilson?' he enquired, extending his right hand as he spoke. 'Harper-Brown's the name. I've been asked to take you to Thessalonika. If you'd like to come this way I've got a car waiting.'

He picked up Ray's bag and turned towards the road and a waiting Jaguar XF, in which the driver had kept the engine running to maintain the air-conditioning. As Harper-Brown put his bag in the boot, Ray was surprised to notice that the car carried diplomatic registration plates. Inside, his surprise turned to amazement as Harper-Brown handed him a sealed A5 envelope. 'This is your ticket. BA — Club class, naturally — to Heathrow. You will need to ring your Mr Greenwood as soon as you land.' he said. 'Flight time is about three and a half hours and we've got about a two hour drive so I suggest you just relax, take in the views or have a snooze if you want to.'

Ray wasn't even told the driver's name and he got the distinct impression that Harper-Brown was not in the mood for small talk so put his mind to thinking what on earth could have happened that necessitated his recall from holiday. He had no outstanding enquiries and he hadn't been in the West Yorkshire force long enough for a cold-case review to be an issue. Could it be something in his previous job? Hardly. Arts and Antiques were pretty uncontroversial. After half an hour or so his mind gave up and he dropped off to sleep.

He was awakened by Harper-Brown's voice. 'Mr Wilson, we're here. Come with me and I'll take you through.'

Inside the airport, he was taken to a BA check-in desk where his ticket was checked, his bag taken from him and the clerk wished him a pleasant flight. Harper-Brown then guided him to a side door, along a series of corridors and out directly into the departure lounge, all passport and security formalities by-passed.

'What happened to passport...' he began.

'All part of the service sir,' interrupted Harper-Brown. 'Now, if you'd like to go to Gate 64, your aircraft is waiting.' He extended his hand and added. 'Very nice to meet you and good luck in whatever it is you're about to undertake.'

Seconds later he had vanished into the press of waiting passengers.

Ray took the opportunity to ring Colin Greenwood. 'Ah! Wilson,' said the Chief Constable. 'I trust you've had a pleasant journey so far. Now listen, when you get to London, you will be taken to meet someone who has a special job he wants you to do.'

'What kind of job sir?'

'I can't tell you any more than that Wilson. Except to say that you don't have to accept it. You can come back here without a blemish on your record. But if you do accept, you will be beyond my control and more importantly, beyond my help. The decision is yours and yours alone. Do you understand?'

'It sounds a bit theatrically cloak-and-dagger sir, if you don't mind me saying so,' said Ray. 'But, yes, I fully understand. Thank you sir.'

When he reached Gate 64, a pretty Greek girl in a BA uniform greeted him with: 'Good Afternoon Mr Wilson. I hope you have an enjoyable flight' and waved him into the air-bridge without checking either his boarding card or passport. Someone, somewhere had been pulling strings. He was obviously expected and was being identified by people he didn't know from Adam. When he reached the aircraft's doors he was met by two smiling BA cabin crew, who also greeted him by name. And then he did something he had never done in his life before. He turned left into Club Class.

As he took his seat next to the window he couldn't help but notice there was no one else in the compartment, but before he could give it a second thought, a tall, willowy stewardess arrived at his side, her nut-brown hair swept into a knot at the back of her head. 'Welcome aboard Mr Wilson,' she said. 'We'll be boarding the other passengers now and we should be on our way to London soon. In the meantime, would an MSG go down well?'

'An MSG?' queried Ray?

'Yes sir. A Man Sized Gin.'

'You read my mind,' he replied with a grin.

***

Three and half hours and two more MSGs later, the aircraft dropped through a cloudy sky onto Heathrow's main runway and taxied up to Terminal 5. There was a delay of five minutes or so before the air-bridge was connected and the aircraft's doors opened, by which time Ray had been ushered to the front of the queue of disembarking passengers. Inside the terminal, he realised the reason for the delay.

At the end of the air-bridge were two men, both in civilian clothes, one of them holding his luggage. 'Mr Wilson, come with us please,' said the bag carrier. There were no introductions, no pleasantries, just business-like efficiency. Ray suddenly knew what it felt like to be arrested as the two men, both of them larger than he was, took station on either side of him and rapidly walked him out through a side door and down a steel staircase to where another Jaguar awaited. He climbed into the back with one of the men alongside him and the other in the front passenger seat. As the car pulled away, the man sitting on his right said: 'Nothing to worry about Mr Wilson. We just had to make sure that you weren't observed at Customs.'

'Er...I don't understand,' said Ray. 'Why should I not be seen at Customs?'

'I'm afraid I don't know the answer to that sir,' said his travelling companion, unconvincingly. 'We just do what we're told.'

'So where are you taking me?'

'Just into town sir. You'll see soon enough.'

Realising he wasn't going to get a straight answer, Ray fell silent and watched the streets of London pass by, through South Kensington and Belgravia until he recognised Buckingham Palace on his left. The car turned ninety degrees right and carried on. A couple more turns and it stopped outside a red-brick building that reminded him of places he'd seen in Holland. Looking up he saw a large chrome sign that only served to deepen the mystery.

It said: 'National Crime Agency.'

CHAPTER 3

All Ray knew about the Agency was what he had read in the newspapers when it came into being in October 2013, hailed by the media as 'Britain's FBI.' It was charged with tackling serious organised crime, strengthening Britain's borders, combating fraud and cyber crime as well as protecting children and young people from sexual abuse and exploitation. The nine former senior — very senior — police officers that made up its executive board were just names to him. He didn't know anybody of any rank who had been recruited and he didn't know anybody of any rank who had voiced the opinion that joining the NCA was a good career move.

And now he stood on the doorstep, holiday bag in hand, unbriefed, unknowing and uncertain of what to expect on the other side of the door. Not a position that policemen of any rank enjoyed being in. He was sure, though, of one thing. They must want something he had very badly indeed, otherwise, why lay on the VIP treatment? While he pondered, the Jaguar and its three occupants drove away without so much as a goodbye. He felt his heart rate rise as he stepped through the door.

On the other side he found himself in a spacious reception area that could have belonged to any major company in any city in the world. Behind a desk sat a single receptionist: female, middle-aged, smartly dressed without being prim. Her very presence said reliable, dependable, trustworthy.

Gently putting his bag on the floor, Ray said: 'Good Afternoon my name is Wilson, DCI Wilson of West Yorkshire Police. The thing is I don't know who I am here to see. In fact, I don't even know why I'm here.'

'Ah, Mr Wilson, welcome, we've been expecting you,' she said. 'Did you have a pleasant journey? Thassos wasn't it? Lovely part of the world.' But before Ray got the chance to answer, she added: 'Take a seat and I'll let them know you're here.'

The words hit him as he sat down. *'I'll let them know...'* So it wasn't one man he was meeting as Greenwood had claimed. There would be at least two of them, maybe more. He struggled to control his runaway imagination as he waited to be summoned. In the end it was no more than a couple of minutes, but it felt like hours, before the receptionist reappeared.

'Will you come with me please Mr Wilson?' she said, turning towards a pair of large, modern light oak doors.

'Do you need to me to sign in or anything?'

'That won't be necessary Mr Wilson. We know where to find you if anything's missing.'

It was a weak attempt at a weak joke that simply passed Ray by. It would take more than a half-hearted wisecrack to detract him from what was churning through his brain. On the first floor, she took him to another large door, knocked once, opened it and stood back saying as she did so: 'Gentlemen, DCI Wilson.' Ray found himself in an airy conference room facing one side of a long, wide table, made from the same light oak as the doors.

On the opposite side of the table sat three men. The middle one stood, motioning Ray to a chair opposite his as he said: 'Mr Wilson, good of you to come. Let me introduce myself and my colleagues. I am Charles Barker, Director of Operations here at the NCA. On my right is Michael Wilpshire, Director of the Organised Crime Command and on my left is Bernard Copeland, Director of the Border Policing Command.

'Now, I expect you're anxious to know why you're here.'

Ray's brow furrowed. 'Yes sir, it has been puzzling me. I wasn't even told I was coming to the NCA.'

'No, I have to admit I didn't understand the need for that particular bit of secrecy, but the important thing is you're here now,' said Barker. 'Let me begin by giving you a bit of background. I'm sure you've read all the guff in the papers about us being Britain's FBI and all that bollocks. But the thing is, we have a very wide ranging brief, we have political support and we have resources.

'Among our high priorities is tackling serious, organised and complex crime threats from abroad, before they reach our shores. That means identifying — and stamping down hard — on those who would seek to disrupt our way of life through smuggling firearms, drugs, cash and, in some cases, even people. To do that we work hand-in-glove with a lot of partners, both in this country and overseas. They include law enforcement agencies, intelligence gathering agencies, various government departments and private civilian sources. I'm sure I don't need to go into detail.

'That task is undertaken by the Border Policing Command, run by Mr Copeland here. He has more than 600 officers at every UK port and airport, plus around 120 international liaison officers covering 150 countries. But by its very nature, the work of the BPC overlaps with that of the Organised Crime Command, which is Mr Wilpshire's responsibility. Any questions so far?'

Again Ray's brow creased in puzzlement. 'Not really sir. It's all very impressive, but I don't understand how it involves me.'

'I'm coming to that Mr Wilson, please bear with me,' replied Barker. 'One of our sources has identified an illegal organisation — I hesitate to use the word "gang," it's much more sophisticated than that — that appears to cover the whole of Europe and parts of the Middle East like a spider's web. According to our source, it is singly responsible for the trafficking into the UK of people, especially young women from Eastern Europe, for the purposes of prostitution. It is also a major supplier of Class A and B drugs and firearms to criminal gangs operating in this country.

'Our understanding is that this organisation is so powerful it has bought itself protection at the very highest level. Do you understand the implications of that statement Mr Wilson?'

'Are you saying that this "organisation" as you describe it, successfully bribes senior police officers in this country?' Ray could barely conceal his disbelief.

'Not just policemen Mr Wilson,' continued Barker. 'Politicians and members of the judiciary may be involved too. What we are dealing with is an insidious, manipulative force for evil that potentially poses the biggest threat to law and order this country has ever seen.'

Struggling to absorb what he had just been told, Ray said: 'I still don't understand what this has to do with me. What you are talking about is way out of my league. I'm just a humble DCI in West Yorkshire.'

Wilpshire, the Director of the Organised Crime Command, jumped in. 'That's precisely why we chose you Mr Wilson. We understand you have experience in undercover work and in infiltrating organised crime gangs in particular.'

'Well, yes I do, but I've only done it once,' answered Ray. 'You must have dozens, if not hundreds, of people in London that have much more experience than me. Why not use one of them?'

'You're right Mr Wilson, we do have many people who, on paper at least, fit the bill better than you,' said Wilpshire. 'But the thing is we have no way of knowing how many of them have been compromised. We don't know if any of them would work against us as a double agent, as it were. And to be quite blunt, we don't know how many of them could be on the take. For all we know, every single one of them could be as honest as the day is long but it's a risk we can't take.

'In other words, we need an unknown face; a face that's not known to the criminals; a face that's not known to the regular agencies and a face that has credibility. We believe that face is you.'

Ray was stunned and not just by the enormity of the task that faced whoever took on the job. He was stunned too by the fact that a newly-formed crime-fighting agency knew enough about a hick copper from the sticks to have him brought back from holiday and trust him enough to want him to infiltrate a gang with very long fingers in very big pies.

For several seconds he sat there looking blank, struggling to find words. Then: 'If — and I emphasise "if" — if I was to take this job, what's in it for me? Give me a reason why I should put my life at risk.'

Barker, who had been sitting with his hands clasped together and pressed to his lips as if in silent prayer, said: 'Frankly Mr Wilson, there's absolutely nothing in it for you. In fact, because HM Government would know nothing about it, it would be a completely deniable exercise. If, for example, you ran into trouble abroad, the Government would be wholly justified in claiming you were acting on your own initiative; as a freelance as it were. There would be no help and no support from them.

'But if your actions proved successful in bringing down this organisation, then an appreciable amount of money would appear in your bank account and you could quietly retire, if that's what you wanted. Or you could simply go back to the hum-drum life of being an ordinary copper. The choice would be yours.'

The Director of Operations let the conversation hang, adding no embellishment or explanation. Instead, he just stared Ray in the eyes.

In the silence, Ray was convinced he could hear his own heart beat. 'You need to tell me more,' he said. 'You haven't given me enough information for me to able to form an opinion. I need to know what the job will involve, who the targets are, what back-up I'd have, reporting systems, extraction procedures if things go tits-up, that kind of thing. I can't be expected to make a decision of this magnitude based on what you've told me today.'

'We appreciate that,' said Barker. 'That's why we've taken the liberty of booking you into an hotel for tonight so you can come back first thing tomorrow and have a full briefing from Mr Copeland. Only when that briefing is complete will we ask you for a decision. Just bear in mind that once you have made your decision, there can be no turning back. Do you understand?'

'Yes sir. Totally.'

'Fine. If you'd like to wait in reception, I'll get someone to take you to your hotel. The reservation is in your name and the bill will be taken care of. A car will collect you at 0830 sharp tomorrow. Now, enjoy your evening. Goodbye Mr Wilson.'

'Er...thank you gentlemen. Goodbye.'

■■

When the Jaguar with its driver and attendant "passengers" picked him up, Ray's immediate fear was it would take him to one of the many small hotels in the area favoured by penny-pinching Whitehall departments. He was amazed therefore to realise that the car was heading up Whitehall towards Trafalgar Square, then onto the Strand before it made a left turn into Aldwych and stopped outside what he recognised as being a five-star hotel, a place about which he had read glowing reviews in the Sunday papers.

At the reception desk he was greeted like a favoured and influential guest, handed the key to his room and a plain white envelope, on which his name had been written in near-perfect copper-plate by someone using a fountain pen.

In his room, he casually threw his travel bag on to the king-sized bed and ripped open the envelope. Inside he found £250 in unused £20 and £10 notes and a note, written by the same hand that had addressed it. The note simply read: 'I thought you might need some spending money in Sterling — Barker.' It was a gesture that underlined, superficially at least, that the NCA's Director of Operations had been telling the truth when he said it was an organisation with resources.

Ray glanced at his watch and realised it was early evening and he had eaten nothing that day except airline food — in Business Class true, but it was still airline food — and that had been six hours earlier. He showered, changed into clean clothes and took the lift back to the ground floor and the hotel's tasteful, spacious bar. He took a stool at the bar and noticed that around him, the majority of people were drinking garishly coloured cocktails from elegant glasses. At least one of the drinks he saw appeared to be smoking.

His eyes roamed over the collection of bottles behind the bar, searching for something less exotic and more suited to his palate. Almost a minute had passed before he spotted it, a 25 year-old Talisker, the only single malt made on the Isle of Skye. He had to try it, no matter what the cost — and he had no illusions that it would be anything other than eye-watering. After all, he could simply put it on his bill. Or he could use a chunk of Barker's £250.

In the end he decided to part with the cash, then spent several minutes just admiring the caramel-coloured liquid and swirling it around the heavy-bottomed tumbler. He added a tiny splash of cold water, put his nose to the glass and savoured the aroma of seaweed, smoke and, distantly, oranges. Then he put the glass to his lips and took a sip. The initial sweetness rapidly gave way to saltiness and a toasty, almost peppery finish. It was, he decided, probably the best whisky he had ever tasted.

'You look like you're enjoying that.'

Ray had been so absorbed in the Talisker he hadn't noticed the woman who had sat down on the stool alongside him. She was mid to late 30s, blonde hair — which he could see was not her natural colour — fashionably and expensively cut, wearing a light grey two-piece suit and a pale yellow blouse that had a tantalising but not revealing neckline.

'It's beautiful. There's no other word for it,' he replied. Only he knew whether he was referring to the whisky or the view.

'What is it?' she enquired.

'It's twenty-five year-old Talisker single malt. From the Isle of Skye,' he said. 'I've had the 10 year-old and the 18 before but the 25 is a rare thing to find behind a bar.'

'Sounds interesting,' she said. 'I was going to treat myself to a cocktail but I think I might try one of those instead.'

24

'Good choice. Let me get it. And you need a splash of cold water in it. Releases a whole complex of flavours.' The words came out before he even had a chance to think about them.

'That's very kind of you,' she said, putting up no argument whatsoever. 'My name's Sally by the way, Sally O'Dwyer. My parents obviously didn't give a sod when they named me.' It struck Ray as an introduction worn by use but he still managed to raise a smile.

'I'm Ray. Ray Wilson. So tell me Sally O'Dwyer, what brings you to this super-cool establishment? Meeting someone?'

'No. I'm all alone. I was on my way home from work and I was bitten by the urge for strong drink and decided this would be a nice classy place to take it. What about you?'

'Actually, I'm staying here tonight. On business.'

'It must be a lucrative business if they can afford to put you up here. What do you do?'

'I'm a yacht broker,' Ray lied. 'Basically, hotels like this are part of the charade. I need to be seen in the top places. And what's your line?'

'I work in an insurance office, in Fleet Street, just at the other end of The Strand.'

'Aha. The Street of Adventure — or The Street of Shame, depending on your point of view.'

'Sorry, I'm not with you.

'When national newspapers were in their heyday, Fleet Street was where they were all based,' Ray explained. 'The guys who worked there referred to it as The Street of Adventure after an early 20th century novel about newspapers. But Private Eye, the satirical magazine, called it The Street of Shame in a regular column that exposed the short-comings of the journalists who worked there.'

'Were you one of them then?'

Another lie tripped from his tongue. 'No, no. Not at all. But my older brother was a reporter for the Daily Express in the seventies and eighties. He calls it the Belle Epoch; before the bean counters ruined it all.'

'I'm afraid I don't read newspapers,' said Sally. 'I get all the news I need from television and the internet.'

'You're not alone there,' said Ray. 'Although I don't think newspapers will ever die out completely, people will just change the way they read them.'

Sensing that Sally was finding talk of newspapers boring, he ventured: 'So tell me, does your insurance company provide cover for yachts? My clients often ask me if I can recommend a good insurance company.'

She shifted slightly on the stool. 'I'm not 100 per cent sure about that,' she said. 'My speciality is risk management. We insure overseas investments, that kind of thing.'

'Sounds interesting.'

'No it's not. Tell me about yachts. Have you got one?'

'Afraid not,' said Ray. 'But I do love sailing. I race on other people's yachts whenever I get the opportunity.'

'That sounds exciting. Where do you race? The Solent?'

'All over the place really. It depends where I am, what's on and who I know who can get me a ride.'

Over the next hour, the pair chatted about inconsequential things. Ray told her more about his passion for sailing. She told him about her love of horses. They established that both were unattached romantically. And more Talisker disappeared down their throats.

Finally Ray said: 'Look, I only flew back from Greece today and apart from what I was given on the plane, I haven't eaten. I was going to get something here. Would you like to join me?'

Sally stared deeply into his eyes. 'Yes. I'd like that very much. There's a lovely little Italian place not far away. Why don't we go there instead? It will be a bit quieter — and cheaper.'

'Lead on Ms O'Dwyer,' he said, climbing off the stool and offering her his hand.

***

She was right about the Italian. It was small, intimate, only half-full and reasonably priced. A bottle of Barolo washed down fettuccini followed by veal and left Ray with a distinctly mellow feeling. The hotel was barely five minutes' walk away. His room had a king-sized bed. He knew that sex was a probability, not a possibility. All he had to do was ask.

But yet.

Something was not quite right. Something in Sally's body language disturbed him. Something in his own mind jangled alarm bells. He couldn't identify what was wrong. He just knew something was.

He paid the bill and as they left he gently said to her: 'Look, I've had a really, really nice time tonight but I've been travelling all day and I'm dead on my feet. I need to get some sleep. Can I meet you again tomorrow? After work?'

'It's OK, I understand,' she said. 'Be in the bar at six. If I can make it, I'll be there before six-thirty. If I don't make it, call me.' She pushed a card into his hand. 'My mobile number's on there. Good night and thank you.'

She stretched and kissed him gently on the cheek, then turned away and walked towards a taxi rank.

CHAPTER 4

The following morning the car he had been promised would collect him at 8.30 arrived on the second. There were perfunctory greetings from the three men inside but no further conversation as the car headed for NCA headquarters. Ray watched fascinated as the driver expertly picked his way through the rush-hour traffic, taking care not to get boxed in or to get too close to the vehicle in front, avoiding the middle lane, always leaving himself an escape route. It was text book-perfect driving from a man thoroughly trained in evasive and defensive techniques.

They left Ray on the NCA's doorstep and drove off without a word. Inside, the same receptionist greeted him with a smile, made a brief call in which she said only: 'Mr Wilson's arrived' and then ushered him once more to the first floor. This time though, he was shown into the office of Bernard Copeland, Director of Border Policing Command. Copeland's secretary led him to a small meeting room, simply furnished with a round table, four hardback chairs and a wooden cabinet.

'Mr Copeland will be with you shortly,' she said, closing the door behind her and leaving Ray to stare at the four walls. He hadn't got further than a print of JMW Turner's painting "The Fighting Temeraire" when Copeland burst in and dropped a heavy box file in the table.

'Wilson, good to see you,' he said. 'Did you have a pleasant evening? Nice hotel that. You meet some interesting people in there.'

'Yes thank you sir. Very pleasant,' Ray replied, images of Sally flickering through his brain.

'Right. Down to business,' said Copeland, producing a thick bound document from within the box file. 'I don't expect you to have made a firm decision overnight on the basis of what you were told yesterday. I want you to read this, absorb it and then tell me whether you're in or out. If you're in, we'll go to the next level. If you're out, then you'll be sent back to West Yorkshire. Either way, there will be no mention of this on your record. As Mr Barker told you, this operation will remain totally deniable.'

Ray could see the document was titled: "Operation Hydra: Briefing Document," but other than that, there was no clue as to what might lie within it.

Copeland tapped it with his index finger. 'This document contains everything we know about the organisation that was outlined to you yesterday. I can't let you take it out of this room and no part of it can be copied so, if you don't mind, I'd like your mobile phone please. I assume it has a camera?'

Ray handed over his phone without a word.

'Read it carefully. It will probably take you a couple of hours. Just tell my secretary when you've finished it and we'll meet up again,' Copeland said. 'Oh and just one more thing Wilson. If you want tea, coffee or a sandwich or something, Alice — that's my secretary — will get it for you. You are not to leave this room. If you need the toilet, Alice will lock the document in her safe and accompany you. I know that's all a bit melodramatic, but you'll see the reasons for it when you read what's in it.'

As Copeland left, Ray took off his jacket, hung it over the back of his chair and began reading.

The operation had been codenamed Hydra because the organisation it described was a many-headed beast that dealt solely in human misery. Its known activities were the importation, supply and distribution of drugs; the supply of firearms and other ordnance, including plastic explosives and the supply of false documents, including passports, visas and residency permits. The individual "branches" of the organisation worked in cells, each one unknown to the next, so that even when police arrested members of one cell, the main body of the beast remained intact and other heads were soon recruited to start all over again.

The organisation's particular speciality was in people trafficking with one estimate claiming it brought as many as 100 people a week into the UK in an on-going operation that used a variety of ports of entry and many different methods.

From among that human cargo, the organisation targeted young women who it forced to become sex workers in the string of brothels, lap dancing clubs and "hostess bars" it operated throughout the UK and Europe.

But most chilling of all was evidence that the organisation had influence over politicians, judges, lawyers and senior police officers, each of whom had been caught by the oldest trick in the book, the honey trap. The prettiest of the women it had forced into prostitution were compelled to use their charms on senior members of the Establishment, who were then blackmailed with threats of revealing photographs and voice recordings. It never failed.

The head of the organisation was identified as Michael Pilling, owner of a trans-European transport business based in Colchester, Essex, which specialised in carrying cargo to and from the UK, as far afield as Turkey. It was the perfect cover for the organisation's activities, especially as Michael Pilling was not too particular about whom he employed and seemed to prefer men who had criminal records.

An example of the extent of the hold the organisation had on the judiciary and the police was the case of Frank Chiswell, one of its enforcers who had been arrested and charged with murder after the naked body of an 18 year-old Romanian girl was found lashed to a pier piling in Southend. She had been eviscerated.

Chiswell was indentified from CCTV images that showed him carrying something wrapped in a sheet on to Southend beach in the early hours of one morning at low tide. Her body was not discovered until after the following high tide receded. Police believed her "crime" was to refuse to have sex with the 24-stone Chiswell and charged him with her murder.

However, a judge granted him bail, his passport was returned to him, his fingerprints and DNA were mysteriously wiped from the national databases and a Stop and Detain Order issued to all ports and airports was cancelled. Chiswell was believed to have flown out of the country in a light aircraft and was now one of the organisation's fixers in Holland.

Ray reached the end of the document and rocked back on his chair. He remembered the paintings he had studied when he was taking his history of art degree; paintings that depicted Hercules killing the Hydra as the second of his 12 Labours. According to legend the Hydra lived in the Swamps of Lerna, from where it terrorised the local population while guarding an entrance to the Underworld. It was said that one of its nine heads was immortal and that if any head was cut off, two more would grow in its place. Hercules eventually completed his task with the help of his nephew Iolaus who used a flaming torch to seal the neck after Hercules had decapitated it. He lopped off the immortal head with a golden sword and buried it, still spitting and snarling, under a huge rock.

Now all he had to do was stand in the footsteps of Hercules. It didn't auger well for the mission Ray was facing.

If he took this on, it would be a massive, massive task that unless he got a lucky break could take years to complete. It would also be very dangerous on a personal level. This organisation clearly had no compunction about using violence and if his secret was uncovered he knew his death would be slow and painful.

But if something wasn't done, the sway the organisation held over the British way of life would only get bigger and would probably pose a more serious threat than any terrorist gang.

His mind was made up.

He opened the door and spoke to Alice, who was at her desk drinking herbal tea from a China cup.

'Will you please tell Mr Copeland I've finished the document?' he asked.

It was another ten minutes before Copeland appeared. 'Right Wilson,' he began, 'I understand you have read the document. As I said, it covers pretty much everything we know but if you have any questions I'll do my best to answer them.'

'I'm in,' was all Ray said.

'What?'

'I said I'm in.'

'Just like that?'

'Just like that.'

'You are aware of the risks — no, of the dangers — that are inherent with this mission?

'Yes sir, perfectly. But it's a job that has to be done and if it all goes wrong, well, I don't have any family and there's no one close to me. I'm on my own.'

Copeland stared at him for several seconds. 'I have to say Mr Wilson' — Ray noted the change in the way he was addressed — 'that it's a very brave decision. Like we told you yesterday, we had already decided you were our man and I was ready to give you the old patriotic speech about defending England from the criminal menace. I'm delighted that that's not necessary. Now...'

'Before we go any further,' Ray interrupted, 'there are a couple of conditions. If they can't be met, I'm walking.'

'OK. Let's hear them.'

'First of all, I want a liaison officer I know and can trust,' said Ray. 'There's a DS on my team in West Yorkshire called Jan Holroyd. I want her. She's to be given Acting Detective Inspector rank, with all the consequent pay and pensions increases. And she's to be given a single point of contact here at the NCA. No one below the level of Director. I want to reduce the dangers she will be in to the absolute minimum.

'Secondly, The NCA will pay my mortgage and ensure that my home is properly looked after and maintained for as long this takes. If that means getting one of your people to live there, so be it.'

'Anything else?' asked Copeland.

'That's it for now. If I think of anything else, I'll let you know.'

'Fine. We can do all that. I'll get in touch with West Yorkshire straight away. Oh, and well done on not rising to the bait.'

A puzzled expression creased Ray's face.

'The bait? I don't know what you're talking about.'

'I think you do Mr Wilson.'

Copeland closed the meeting room door behind him.

CHAPTER 5

Ray glanced again at his watch, the fifth time in as many minutes. It was close to 7.00pm, almost half an hour after she said she'd be there. She wasn't going to make it. He swallowed what was left of his 25 year-old Talisker and walked out into the hotel lobby where he rang the mobile number on the card she had given him the previous night.

It went straight to voicemail: 'Hi, this is Sally. You know what to do.'

It was in that instant Ray recognised the doubts he had felt the previous evening and he knew immediately what the problem had been. Sally was a set-up. She was the bait Copeland had referred to. In the same way the Hydra lured and compromised its high-ranking victims, the NCA had tried to entice him into a honey trap.

Fury boiled in his blood. It was obvious they didn't really trust him. They could stuff their job up their arses. If this was how they treated people, he didn't want to know. He would go back to being a provincial copper. His first reaction was to throw his mobile against a wall, an urge he resisted only because there were other people around. Then he wanted to shout out loud, another urge he resisted because of his surroundings. Finally, he decided the sensible thing to do was gather some proof before he started making accusations.

He walked out of the hotel, turned right and then left onto The Strand. He carried on walking past St Clement Danes — the Central Church of the Royal Air Force, where the church clock plays "Oranges and Lemons" four times day — past the Royal Courts of Justice and into Fleet Street. After five minutes searching he identified the building in which, according to her business card, Sally O'Dwyer worked. It was an insurance company sure enough, but not the one named on the card. Nor did the firm's name appear on the brass plaque that listed all the associated companies. Ray's police brain told him it was evidence but not proof. Ray's heart told him it was enough.

He rang Bernard Copeland from outside Ye Olde Cheshire Cheese. The Director had said only 'Mr Wilson' when Ray gave him both barrels. It began with: 'You lying bastards. How dare you set me up...'

and went on, unabated, for a full minute until it reached: 'And you can stick your job where the sun doesn't shine. I quit.'

***

Sitting at home with a cup of tea in his hand, watching some idiotic game show on television, Bernard Copeland let Ray rant uninterrupted until he yelled: 'I quit.'

'Mr Wilson, please let me explain,' he began. 'Believe me, we didn't set you up. You haven't been spied on or enticed and me describing Sally as "bait" was clumsy to say the least. She's one of my best agents and I sent her to the hotel to make sure you weren't set-up, as you put it. Her brief was merely to keep an eye on you; to make sure no one got to you. As you now know, Hydra has tentacles everywhere and we had to be sure that no one put temptation of any kind in your way. Sally was following orders and she would have done anything to make sure no one else got near you. Except you said were tired and wanted to go to sleep.'

'So why the fake ID,' yelled Ray. 'Why couldn't she be honest with me?'

'Come off it Wilson.' Ray didn't notice the Mr had been dropped. 'Anybody could have been listening, accidentally or on purpose. Any mention of the NCA would cause ears to prick up. And it's not a fake ID, well, not wholly fake anyway. Only her occupation and her employers are false. It's her cover. Remember that? Cover?'

Ray had calmed down, but only slightly. 'I still think it was a shit's trick and I think it shows you don't really trust me. So I quit. I'm going home.'

'Bit late for that Wilson,' Copeland replied impassively. 'Acting Detective Inspector Holroyd is already on her way here. Just think how disappointed she would be — not to mention embarrassed — at having to return to her old job and her old rank after less than 24 hours. The car will pick you up at 0830 again.'

The line went dead as Copeland hung up.

***

The rumour mill began turning within minutes of the note being circulated in the Major Incident Team office in Bradford. Signed by Colin Greenwood, West Yorkshire's Chief Constable, it said merely that Detective Chief Inspector Raymond Wilson and Detective Sergeant

Janice Holroyd were detached with immediate effect and would not be returning to duty for the foreseeable future.

'I knew it. I knew there were something dodgy between them two,' ventured Peter Barnes, the youngest detective on the team. 'They've been suspended I bet.'

'I think you're wrong there,' countered Paul Prendergast. 'If they'd been suspended the Chief would have said so. And anyway, what would they have been suspended for? Being good at the job? No, I reckon it's something in their personal lives.'

Mark Blake said: 'Do you think they were that close? I don't. It was obvious the Boss thought the sun shone out of Jan's arse but I don't think he fancied her; he was too focused on the job. Then again, who knows what went on out of the office, eh?'

'They could have eloped,' added Barnes. 'Done a runner like.'

'Bloody hell Barnsey, I sometimes wonder what you've got that passes for a brain,' said Blake. 'The clue's in the note. It says they are "detached" and to my mind that means they've been sent off to do something else. The powers that be just don't want us to know what it is.'

The speculation formed the main topic of conversation all day. Every member of the team put forward their own theories as to where the Boss and Jan Holroyd had gone and for what purpose.

None of them came close to the truth.

***

Back in Fleet Street, Ray decided that Ye Old Cheshire Cheese — originally opened in 1538 and rebuilt after the Great Fire of London in 1666 — was as good a place as any to begin his search for insensibility. Inside, the virtual lack of natural light gave the pub an oddly welcoming gloominess. Once the haunt of journalists and tourists by the score, the bar he found himself in had just six patrons, two men standing at the bar and two couples sitting at a corner table. A sad sign of the times.

He ordered a pint of bitter and found his own dark corner in which to contemplate his future. One pint didn't do it, so he had another and then another. He still hadn't made his mind up what to do when he wandered across Fleet Street to The Tipperary, said to be the first Irish pub in London, where he downed a couple of pints of Guinness. Clarity still hadn't struck so he walked further along the street to The Old Bell, where he squeezed through a herd of braying suits to order his sixth pint of the evening.

He liked The Old Bell. The place obviously had history and, like many pubs in the area, had two entrances, one front and one back. The bar was almost oval and set in the middle of the floor, leaving lots of room for guests to stand and drink. Ray's only problem was with his fellow drinkers who seemed to be engaged in a competition to see who could speak the loudest in the most ridiculous accents. He voted the suit that was trumpeting about its wife spending an "Arr in the sharr" to be the winner. He had to leave before he punched someone.

By now it was gone 10pm and time, Ray decided, to return to the hotel. Outside, he miraculously spotted a cab that was still working. Five minutes later he was back in the hotel bar, sipping a gin and tonic and feeling very sorry for himself, still not having made his mind up about what to do. He would vaguely remember ordering one more — and then the next thing he knew, his alarm was none-too-gently reminding him it was time to get up.

***

By the time the car dropped him once more outside the NCA headquarters, Ray was feeling a bit rough around the edges and with uncertainty about the direction in which his future lay chewing at him from the inside out. Did he stick to his guns and insist that he wanted nothing more to do with the NCA and Hydra? Or should he be contrite, apologise for his behaviour and just get on with the job?

As he walked through the door, all choices evaporated. He instantly knew there was only one course of action because sitting there waiting for him was Jan Holroyd. The first thought that crossed Ray's mind was that the black two-piece suit she was wearing looked very expensive for a detective sergeant's salary, a chauvinist notion he rapidly dismissed. The suit was complemented by a royal blue blouse in a shiny material that his mere male mind could not identify, over which was a discreet gold chain. Black suede shoes with kitten heels gave her a dignified, business-like appearance. A flush of pride coursed through him.

The second she spotted him Jan jumped to her feet, rushed towards him, threw her arms around his neck and gave him a big kiss on the cheek, taking him aback. It was not the kind of reception he normally got from junior officers.

'Great to see you Guv,' she said. 'How's it going? Did you have a good holiday? What're we doing here?' The excitement poured from her in a torrent.

'Whoa, whoa, *Detective Inspector* Holroyd,' said Ray, emphasising her new rank. 'One thing at a time. You're here because I asked for you. You'll find out why in due course. First job is for you to meet your new bosses and then we can get started on the proper job.'

'And what might that be then?'

'In a nutshell, it involves an international crime organisation that's into just about every criminal activity you can think of. And it's been getting away with it because it's bought itself friends in some very high places,' Ray told her. 'My job — our job — is to bring about its downfall. Simple as that.'

Jan's big brown eyes were wide open. 'Shit Guv. I should've stayed in Bradford. I'm not up to this kind of malarkey.'

'Yes you are Jan,' he replied. 'I wouldn't have asked for you if I didn't think you were up to it.'

***

Upstairs, once again in Copeland's office, Ray tried to offer his apologies for the previous evening to the Director of Border Policing Command. He had got no further than: 'Look, sir, about last night...' when Copeland held up his right hand, as if he were directing traffic. 'Forget it Mr Wilson,' he said. 'It was as much my fault as yours. I should have kept my mouth shut.'

Jan caught the eye of Michael Wilpshire, Director of Organised Crime Command, who gave her an uncomprehending smile that said at least she wasn't the only one who didn't understand the exchange. Before it got chance to develop, Wilpshire said: 'OK Mr Wilson, you do the introductions and then we can get on with things.'

Handshakes over, Wilpshire continued: 'As I see it, the earlier we can get stuck into this job the better. It's going to be a long one and there's no point in prolonging it unnecessarily so I think we should leave it to Mr Wilson to brief DI Holroyd on what we already know about Hydra and carry on with the background that will be essential to the success of the operation.

'We have created a back-story for you Wilson that basically involves a change of name — we'll let you chose it because it has to be memorable and checkable — and a CV that wouldn't make your mother proud. You will see that you are ex-armed forces and a recently released prisoner. You've served six years in prison for assaulting a senior officer. While you were inside, you've become something of a dab hand at IT and, thanks to the Army, you're also a Class One HGV licence holder.

'When you have chosen a cover name that will stand up to scrutiny let me know and I'll organise a passport, driving licence, credit cards, all that sort of thing.'

He handed Jan a spiral bound document. 'It's all in here Holroyd. Your first job is to make sure that Wilson here knows it backwards, upside down and inside out. While you're doing that, we'll get someone to find a place for you to live close to where Wilson will be based. You will report directly to Mr Copeland or to me in his absence but to no one else. Understood?'

'Yes sir, perfectly,' said Jan.

'Good. Any questions?'

'Just one sir,' said Ray. 'I haven't got an HGV licence and they can take years to get. How do we get round that?'

Copeland jumped in. 'Don't worry Mr Wilson. You will have one. We can by-pass all the usual requirements and you will be given an intense course in handling an articulated vehicle so that, should you need it, you won't make a total tit of yourself.

'Now, I suggest we crack on. We've allocated you a small office on the ground floor. You will not be allowed to take any documents — and that includes the one you're holding Holroyd — from the building. Everything must be returned to my secretary at the end of each day.

'Oh and one more thing... You're both staying in the same hotel but it can't go on indefinitely so you need to get through this as quickly as possible. I'm sure the Taxpayers Alliance would not be too happy to learn that the public at large has been paying for two undercover officers to live it up in a five-star hotel. Right let's get on with it.'

At that, both men stood shook hands with Ray and Jan and walked out.

For a few seconds Jan wore an expression of shock and disbelief. 'Bloody hell Guv, this is some serious shit,' she finally said. 'Proper secret squirrels job by the sound of it.'

'I told you it was big,' Ray replied. 'By now you must be beginning to understand why I need a back-up I know and can trust. Let's go and get a brew then we'll find this office we've been given and make a start.'

***

They spent the early part of that evening in the hotel bar. As a nod to Copeland's request to keep costs as reasonable as possible, Ray had down-graded his favourite 25 year-old Talisker to a 16 year-old one. Jan had chosen a cocktail called One D.O.M which, according to the drinks menu, consisted of Benedictine, vodka, fresh lime, honey, lime leaves and egg white. Her only comment was: 'Wow.'

They were sitting at a table from where Ray could see the door, which he constantly surveyed, hoping beyond hope that Sally O'Dwyer might just walk through it again. He clung to the hope through another round of drinks, even though he knew that she had been a plant, a set-up and that the chances of their paths ever crossing a second time were remote to say the least.

For a good half hour Jan had been talking to him, but her voice was nothing more than a background hum as she struggled to get Sally off his mind. Eventually, he turned to Jan. 'I'm hungry. Fancy something to eat? There's a little Italian place just round the corner that's excellent. My treat.'

'In that case Guv, it would be rude not to,' she answered.

The restaurant was busy but not full and they were quickly seated in a discreet corner. Ray ordered exactly what he had eaten when he was here with Sally: fettuccini for starter, followed by veal. He also ordered the same bottle of Barolo without asking Jan for her preference. She followed his lead and ordered the same food.

'You been here before Guv?' she asked. 'The waiter looked like he recognised you.'

'Only once. On my first night in the hotel. It was recommended to me.' Lowering his voice to a barely audible whisper, he added: 'Oh and by the way, don't call me Guv. We don't want to draw attention to ourselves so call me Ray. I know you've got your new rank but technically, we're not police officers any more, we're NCA agents.'

Jan grinned. 'OK Guv, er, sorry, Ray. It won't be easy but I'll do my best.'

They spent the rest of the evening making small talk so inconsequential that the following morning Ray couldn't remember a single thing they had discussed. Back at the hotel, he gave Jan a quick peck on the cheek and went to bed but with thoughts of Sally racing through his head.

***

For the next five days they worked 10 hours a day ensuring that Ray absorbed every minute detail of the back-story the NCA had prepared for him. For his cover name he chose to keep Ray and adopted the surname Welbourne. David Welbourne had been Ray's best friend at school. They spent years together, bruising shins and skinning knees in boyhood adventures across the Fens but they hadn't seen each other since they day they walked out of school, aged 16.

But the memory of daredevil exploits was not the reason he picked the name. David Welbourne had a twin brother called Raymond. And he had died from meningitis when he was one year old. It was the perfect cover for his new identity.

For the rest of the back-story, Ray had been born and brought up in Cambridge. He had not excelled academically and left school with no qualifications worth a light. After a series of uninspiring jobs — milkman, warehouseman, building site labourer, all of which he was fired from — he joined the army at 18 and became Fusilier Raymond Welbourne, 1st Battalion, Royal Regiment of Fusiliers.

He had been a natural soldier and quickly rose to the rank of sergeant. But in 2008, on his third tour of Afghanistan, something snapped inside him. He got it into his head that his company commander was a bully who was picking on the younger soldiers, making their lives miserable, just because he could.

One night in base camp, emboldened by a few beers, Sergeant Welbourne, searched out the officer and attacked him with a broken bottle, slicing off the top of his left ear. As the injured man writhed on the ground, the NCO continued to kick him and stamp on him until he was subdued by four soldiers. He was brought before a court martial, charged with wounding with intent. He was convicted, sentenced to nine years in a civilian prison and ordered to be dishonourably dismissed from the army, a double stain on his character that would make life on the outside extremely difficult.

By the time Friday came around, Jan was satisfied that Ray knew the back-story as well as he ever would. Mid-afternoon she declared: 'Right Ray. You've got it. I can't fault you anywhere. I think it's time I bought you a beer or three.'

'That's the best invitation I've had all week,' he replied. 'But first, we need to tell Copeland and Wilpshire that we're done.'

The senior commanders were pleased at the progress Ray had made, but Wilpshire poured a dampener on the projected celebrations. 'Don't go drinking too much,' he warned. 'You're off to Bedfordshire in the morning.'

Ray was puzzled. 'Bedfordshire sir? What on earth for?'

'You need an HGV Class One licence don't you? Well, this weekend, you're having your first intensive training weekend,' replied Wilpshire. 'You're going to the Driving Standards Agency's Training and Development Centre at Cardington. It's normally closed at weekends but we've taken it over, just for you. You'll also be there on Monday. Like I said, it's intensive training.'

Ray sensed that Jan was crestfallen at the news there would be no celebration of what she and Ray had achieved. 'Is Jan coming with me?' he asked.

Wilpshire sighed. 'I don't think that would be a good idea Mr Wilson, do you?'

***

The DSA's Training and Development Centre is the place where driving test examiners earn their qualifications. It occupies part of what was once RAF Cardington, the base for Britain's experiments with airships in the early 20th century. Two giant hangars are all that remain as reminders of those pioneering days that came to an abrupt end in 1930 when the R101, which had been built and tested in what was affectionately known as Shed 1, crashed in France on its maiden flight, killing 48 of the 54 people on board.

Ray was some miles from the site when he first saw the hangars still dominating the landscape but in need of preservation and restoration work. Even after all these years of neglect they were an imposing sight. Following printed directions, he eventually made a right turn into a long, tree-lined road that originally led to the main gates of RAF Cardington. At the end of the drive, he made another right turn, parked the hire car and made his way over to the two-storey building that was the hub of the TDC.

Inside he was greeted by the centre's manager, who showed him to a comfortable room on the first floor that had everything he would have expected in a moderately priced hotel. Back downstairs, the manager introduced him to two men sitting drinking coffee who, he was told, would be his instructors.

'Hi, I'm Jim Bromley,' said the larger of the two, standing and extending his hand. 'This is my colleague Ron Monks. We're here to give you a crash course — not literally I hope — in driving HGVs. We haven't been told why you need the knowledge and we're not going to ask. All we do ask is that you give us your full attention at all times. And if there's anything you are uncertain of, just ask. We've got what remains of today plus tomorrow and Monday. It's going to be hard work so I suggest we get started straight away.'

'Lead me to it,' said Ray.

Outside, Ray could see that the TDC covered a large area with a road layout that seemed to mimic every hazard a driver could expect to meet in the real world, including hills, adverse cambers, roundabouts and different road surfaces. There were also open spaces providing plenty room for practising reversing and parking.

Parked on one of the practice spaces were a 44 tonne articulated truck and trailer and a smaller rigid truck.

'You're supposed to have a certain length of experience on rigid vehicles before you can take a test for a Class 1 licence,' explained Bromley. 'Obviously we need to short-circuit that but it would be useful for you to get the feel of a rigid before we put you on the artic. Ron here will show you the ropes.'

For the remainder of the day, Ray drove the 18 tonne truck around and around the TDC's road layout. He did hill starts; he did emergency stops; he manoeuvred around roundabouts; he reversed into open spaces and then again into smaller ones.

Finally Monks said: 'Ok, you seem to have got the hang of it in here. Let's go into town and see how you do there.'

Ray could feel the adrenalin rising as he headed out of the training centre and followed Monks' directions into Bedford. He successfully negotiated the bustling town centre, made his way out of the other side and returned to Cardington.

Back in the bar-restaurant that served as the social centre of the TDC, Monks simple said to Bromley: 'He'll do.'

'Excellent.' Bromley said. 'Right let's get something to eat and then we can get started on the theoretical stuff you need to know to drive the HGV.'

It was close to midnight and Ray was shattered, mentally and physically, by the time he crawled into bed. He was up again by seven and by eight he was behind the wheel of the big artic, repeating the manoeuvres he had done the day before and gradually getting the feel for the monster vehicle. More theoretical lectures came that night and on Monday, Bromley took him once more into the streets of Bedford.

As the light began to fade, he parked the HGV for the last time and Bromley told him: 'That's about as good as you're going to get in the time we've got. You're not perfect but you're not bad either. At least you now know your way around one of these things. Let's have a beer.'

The TDC manager opened the bar and the three of them stood drinking pints and talking of nothing important. True to their word, neither of his instructors asked why he needed their expertise and he volunteered nothing, not even the fact that he was police officer or, as was now the case, an NCA agent.

Tuesday morning found him once again sitting in the Agency's reception area, waiting to be ushered into the presence of Copeland and Wilpshire. When he entered the now familiar first floor office they were both reading a document that turned out to be an assessment of his performance at the TDC.

'Right Mr Wilson,' began Copeland, 'it seems that you've just made the grade. You have enough knowledge and skill to claim that you are the holder of an HGV Class One licence. You have also absorbed your back-story and all the information we currently possess on Hydra, so there's only one thing to do — get yourself accepted into the organisation.'

Both men stood and offered their hands to Ray in a rather abrupt signal that the meeting was at an end. 'Best of luck Wilson,' said Wilpshire. 'I think you're going to need it.'

'Yes sir, thank you sir,' stumbled Ray. 'Before I go I'd like to see Jan again, if that's possible.

'I'm afraid it's not,' Copeland said. 'Agent Holroyd is already in place. There's a new mobile phone waiting for you at reception. It's already got her new number in it.

'And I suggest that for the sake of your cover, just in case someone picks up your phone, she's your girlfriend.'

Before he got the chance to say anything, Ray found himself ushered to the door where he was suddenly engulfed by the feeling that he'd been abandoned. Like a lamb to the slaughter, was the expression that crossed his mind.

CHAPTER 6

He found Pilling Transport easily enough. It occupied a site on the outskirts of Colchester, within shouting distance of the A120, the main link road to the port of Harwich. Surrounded by a 15-foot high chain link fence topped by razor wire, it was not the kind of place that invited further inspection, an impression reinforced in Ray's mind by security cameras every 100 feet and huge spotlight gantries on either side of the main entrance and in the yard.

Carrying a small canvas holdall that was not much more than a survival kit — it contained clean underwear, a shirt, socks, toilet bag and a well-thumbed paperback novel — he strode unchallenged through the gate and across the empty yard. To his left there was what appeared to be a maintenance shed adjoining a warehouse and in front of him a single storey office building attached to another large shed, the purpose of which he could not define.

He passed through a door marked "Reception" into a medium sized office, complete with counter that was heated to the kind of temperature habitual to people who never spend time outdoors. It was cloying, suffocating and pervaded by the aroma of cheap perfume. The only occupant was a young woman, probably in her early 20s, wearing a thick, shapeless jumper with jeans tucked inside sheepskin boots. She glanced up from a laptop computer as Ray entered.

'Yeah? Can I help?' She made no attempt to rise from her desk or establish eye contact, content to speak over a distance of 20 feet or so. The girl's apparent indifference immediately caused Ray to question the professionalism of the entire company and he was struck by the contrast between this welcome and the one he had received on his first visit to the NCA headquarters.

'Yeah I hope so. I was wondering if there were any jobs going.'

'What? Here?' It struck Ray as a pointless question but he resisted the urge to make a smart-arse reply.

'Yeah,' was all he said.

'Dunno,' came the response. 'I'll have to check with Mike.'

'Who's Mike?'

'He's the boss.'

He realised that getting any sort of coherent reply from this girl was going to be close on impossible so he said nothing and simply put his bag on the counter as she disappeared through a door at the back of the office.

Two or three minutes passed before she returned. 'Looks like you might be in luck mate,' she said. 'He says to go through,' nodding towards a flap in the end of the counter.

'Thanks sweetheart,' Ray replied, returning the informality and deliberately brushing close to her as he walked through the door from which she had emerged.

He found himself in an office that did not say Managing Director of an international transport business but more Site Office on a building site. It was about 25 feet square and functionally furnished with a steel desk, several steel filing cabinets and a steel table with six hard-backed chairs. A cheap three-seat sofa was pressed against one wall and on the wall above it was a calendar featuring a photograph of a blonde girl in sky-blue mechanic's overalls, pulled down to expose her breasts, the left one of which was daubed with an oily handprint.

Mike Pilling was sitting in an imitation leather executive chair on the far side of the desk, his piggy eyes fixed on Ray. 'Pull up a chair,' he said, his tone somehow managing to convey a threat rather than an invitation.

The photographs that Ray had seen of Pilling had prepared him for the unpleasant complexion, the wrinkled skin and the close-set eyes which, from this range, he could see were a deep burnished brown, a colour he had seen in higher primates at the zoo.

What they had not prepared him for was the sheer malevolence of his presence. It was as if every atom of his being exuded immorality, depravity and viciousness. His face carried a look that seemed to wish nothing but affliction and suffering to his fellow man. There was nothing about his manner or his appearance that would commend him.

Even though Pilling remained sitting, Ray guessed he was taller than him, probably six foot two or three, and extremely thin — 'There's more meat on a dirty fork,' as Ray's grandmother had been fond of saying.

Without any preamble or attempt at formality, Pilling said: 'Summer tells me you want a job.'

It took Ray a split second to realise that Summer must be the name of the young woman in the outer office. 'Yeah, if you've got one,' he replied.

'Might have. Depends on what you can do.'

'I can do most things.' Ray batted the ball straight back.

'Alright, let's cut the crap,' said Pilling. 'I'm Mike Pilling. The Pilling in Pilling Transport but most people round here call me Mike. Now, what's your name?'

'Welbourne. Ray Welbourne.'

'Right Ray Welbourne. Why do you want to work for me?'

'I suppose I've got some skills you might be able to use,' answered Ray.

'Such as what?' demanded Pilling.

'Well, I can drive an HGV...'

Before he could go any further Pilling interrupted him. 'So can all the blokes that work for me and half the women. What else you got?'

'I can organise stuff. I'm good at that. I can get people to do things, even if they sometimes don't want to.'

'Now that sounds like a skill I could possibly use,' said Pilling, his piggy eyes narrowing. 'Where did you learn that?'

'In the army,' said Ray. 'I was a sergeant; Royal Regiment of Fusiliers but I got kicked out.'

'Kicked out? What for?' Ray could tell his interest was rising.

'I twatted an officer because I thought he was bullying one of my lads.'

'And was he?'

'I never found out. It was enough for me that I thought he was.'

'I like that. I like loyalty. I prize it highly,' said Pilling. 'And what have you been doing since you got kicked out?'

'Time,' said Ray.

'Time?' repeated Pilling.

'Yeah. That officer I twatted, I used a broken bottle. Sliced off the top of his ear. I got nine years for wounding with intent. They let me out after six.'

Pilling's mouth stretched downwards in what could have equally been a smirk or a frown. 'I don't see that as a barrier,' he said. 'In fact, it might even be an asset. It shows me you can take orders without question. You any good with guns?'

Ray managed to look shocked. 'Guns? What's that got to do with working for a transport company?' he said.

'Nothing really. Just a personal interest,' replied Pilling. 'As a solider you must have experience.'

'Oh yeah,' said Ray. 'Sidearms, SA80s, light machine guns, heavy machine guns. All the usual infantry stuff. My lads used to reckon I could shoot the balls of a gnat at 200 yards.'

'You a sniper then?'

'A sniper? No chance,' Ray exclaimed. 'You're nobody's mate as a sniper. The bloke's don't want you near them because of all the fire you attract. And obviously the enemy don't like you because of all the damage you do. And then there's all that lying about not moving, pretending to be a clump of grass or a bush. No, it wasn't a job for me.'

Pilling eyed him carefully. Ray tried to guess whether this unpleasant individual had realised he was lying. A few seconds of silence followed and then: 'So what brings you to Colchester?'

'My girlfriend, she lives here,' Ray replied. 'I can live anywhere so I thought I might as well be close to her.'

'Do you live with her then?' Pilling's questions were getting personal.

'She's my girlfriend not my ball and chain,' said Ray. 'I'm staying in a B and B till I can get a place of my own. I like to be able to come and go without anybody pestering me about where I've been. Sooner I can get a job, sooner I can get my own place.'

Pilling mulled over the answers Ray had given, but not for long.

'Hum,' he began, 'I think I might be able to use a man like you. Pay is four hundred a week for starters but if you do well you'll soon be earning more than that. Start tomorrow morning, eight o'clock; not a minute later, understand? Good, any questions?'

'Just one,' said Ray. 'What will I be doing?'

'Anything I tell you to,' came the response. 'See you in the morning. Close the door behind you.'

In the outer office he found Summer leaning over a table, rearranging some box files. For a micro-second he thought it would be fun to give her backside a playful slap but instantly thought better of it. Getting on the wrong side of somebody who obviously had the boss's ear was not a good way to begin.

So he simply said: 'Thanks for the introduction sweetheart. I'm in. See you in the morning.'

'Best not be late,' she said, without even looking up from her work.

***

The following morning Ray was waiting outside the office building when Summer arrived. He watched as she parked her car and then sauntered across to the office with a look of utter boredom on her face. He noticed that even though it was not yet eight o'clock, she was chewing gum.

'Good morning,' he said breezily.

She gave a grunt that those who understood would have interpreted as: 'Is it?'

He waited until she had unlocked the door then followed her inside.

'We didn't get introduced yesterday,' he said. 'I'm Ray Welbourne.'

'Yeah, I know,' she replied. 'Mike told me. I'm Summer.'

'Yeah, I know. Mike told me,' Ray said. 'But he didn't tell me your last name.'

'It's Long. And before you make any fucking wise cracks I've fucking heard them all. OK?'

'It never even entered my head,' he lied. 'But you have to admit it is an unusual name.'

'It's a fucking stupid name. Since I was about ten all my mates have called me All-ie and that's fucking worse. All-ie Summer Long. All-ie Summer Long. They chant it and think it's really funny but I wish I was called Mary Smith or something.'

'Why don't you change it? You can call yourself what you like. You don't have to stick to the name your parents gave you.' He said.

'There's no chance while my parents are still alive. They'd kill me. All my life they've told me I've got the most beautiful name in the world. It's alright for them they don't have to live with it. They've got proper names.'

'Like what?'

'Malcolm and Joan. Anyway, why am I telling you all this shit? I don't even know you.'

'Because I'm a nice guy who's happy to listen to you whinge,' said Ray.

Her response was brief and blunt: 'Fuck off.'

At which point the living storm cloud that was Mike Pilling strode in. By way of greeting he barked: 'You made my coffee yet All-ie?' Turning to Ray he added: 'Right you, in here.' It was obvious there would be no time wasted on idle chit-chat or friendly banter.

He kicked the office door closed behind them, threw his expensive looking leather jacket on the sofa and threw himself down on top of it. He didn't invite Ray to sit. Instead he started: 'As this is your first day, you can spend the morning having a look round the place, meeting a few people, getting to know a bit about the business. Then this afternoon I've got a little job for you. There's been a delivery of pharmaceuticals come in overnight. A couple of the lads will be repacking them this morning and then later I want you to deliver them to our retailers.'

'What, you have shops as well?' asked Ray.

'Not exactly shops,' said Pilling. 'More like a series of middle men who distribute the products to the end users. But you don't need to know stuff like that. Let me just give you one tip — do as you're told, don't ask too many questions and we'll get on just fine. Got it?'

'Yeah, yeah, sorry,' said Ray. 'First day enthusiasm and all that.'

'OK. Now get out of my sight. Ask Summer to get George Curtis to give you the grand tour. I'll see you this afternoon.'

***

Although George Curtis was physically the opposite of his boss, it was immediately obvious to Ray that he had attended the same charm school. 'He wants me to give the grand fucking tour,' he snarled. 'But there's really fuck-all to see. Seen one truck, you've seen 'em all. We'll start over there.'

He led the way across the yard to the maintenance building that Ray had seen on his first visit. Through the open doors he could see two tractor units, both less than a year old, with their cabs tipped forward to allow a couple of mechanics to tinker with their engines.

To make conversation, Ray said: 'Wow. They look like expensive bits of kit. How many have you got?'

'Enough,' came the curt reply.

'And they go all over Europe do they?'

'Yeah. Turkey's as far as we go these days,' Curtis said. 'We used to go into Iraq but when all those fucking Arabs kicked off a couple of years ago Mike decided it wasn't worth the risk.'

'What do you carry?' Curtis's reply would be interesting.

'Anything anybody wants delivering or collecting,' came the non-committal answer. 'We carry all sorts of shit to wherever it needs to be carried.'

At the far end of the workshop stood a solitary 40-foot trailer from which the sounds of hammering, drilling and sawing could be heard.

'What's going on in there?' Ray asked Curtis.

'What d'you mean?'

'All that banging and clattering.'

'Dunno. I can't hear anything.'

Ray made a mental note but chose not to pursue the point.

He followed Curtis through an internal door into the warehouse that stood alongside the workshop. It was full of packing cases, mostly cardboard but some wooden, stacked on top of each other to a height of about 20 feet. In the centre of the warehouse was a square of heavy duty metal shelving that contained hundreds of parcels that appeared to have been graded by size from top to bottom. The parcels were wrapped in a variety of materials, including black plastic and bubbled, protective wrapping.

After the response to his question about the trailer, Ray picked his words carefully. 'I didn't realise you provided your customers with storage facilities as well.'

'We don't,' said Curtis. 'This is all stuff that's been brought in from the Continent and is waiting for onward shipment throughout the country. We have a fleet of smaller trucks that do that.'

Ray risked: 'So what kind of stuff is it?'

'All sorts,' Curtis replied nonchalantly. 'I don't know what's in everything here but usually we have machine parts, car spares, canned food, that sort of stuff. Stuff that won't go off for a couple of weeks keeping.'

As the pair continued to wander aimlessly through the warehouse, Ray became aware of a series of what looked like trapdoors in the floor, probably designed to give access to services such as water, gas or electricity supplies. The edges of most of them were clogged with dust and the daily detritus of the location, but one was clean. He guessed it had been opened very recently and made a mental note to investigate further when the opportunity arose.

Back outside in the yard Ray naturally headed towards the large shed that was attached to the office block. But Curtis cut him off.

'Right, that's it then. There's nothing more to see,' he said curtly.

'What about that place?' Ray nodded towards the shed.

'That's Mike's. There's nothing in there that's related to the business,' said Curtis. 'He keeps his personal stuff in there.'

'Like what?'

'Nosey bastard aren't you,' snarled Curtis. 'Not that it's anything to do with you but he has a couple of classic cars. He keeps them in there.'

'Classic cars eh? What's he got? I'm a bit of a petrol head on the quiet.'

The response seemed to satisfy Curtis who was much calmer when he said: 'He's got an E-type Jag, a Ferrari something or other and a 1951 Alvis TA21. That's my favourite. It's a beauty.'

'I wouldn't mind having a look at those sometime,' Ray said.

'You'll have to ask Mike. But if I was you I'd wait 'til I'd got my feet under the table a bit more.'

They went back into the office, Curtis completely ignoring Summer and going straight to Mike Pilling's office where he knocked once and walked in unbidden with Ray just a couple of paces behind.

'Right Boss, he's had the tour,' he began, jerking a thumb over his shoulder. 'He asked a few questions, I told him to mind his own fucking business and now we're here.

A smile played across Pilling's face without managing to remove the intrinsic evil in the man.

'Good. Now, I've got a job for you Welbourne and saying it's your first time, I'll get George here to go with you,' he said. 'George I want you to take him on the North London run. You've got the usual four drops. I don't care what order you do them in but they all have to be done today OK? You know the drill. Show him how it's done so he can do the next ones on his own. Take the white Transit.'

**

Curtis took Ray back to the central shelved area in the storage warehouse where he pushed an old supermarket trolley towards him.

'You'll need this. This stuff can get heavy.'

Ray followed the surly giant as he walked slowly around searching the mountain of parcels, occasionally pulling one off the rack and throwing it into the trolley.

The parcels were all roughly the same size, each wrapped in plastic and sealed with black gaffer tape. Ray didn't have to ask what was in them. Even through the thick wrapping he could see that each one contained what appeared to be four bricks and two longer, flatter ones that made a rattling sound.

He surmised the bricks were probably heroin or cocaine and the rattling was probably caused by amphetamine tablets of some kind.

He guessed the entire consignment had a street value in excess of £250,000. And it was being shipped into London in an ordinary Ford van.

Apart from grunting occasional directions, Curtis was silent for virtually the entire journey. It was only as the van approached the outskirts of London that he became animated, constantly scanning side roads and junctions, checking the driving mirror — and Ray's speed.

'Keep your eyes peeled for the Old Bill,' he said more than once. 'And don't do anything that might attract attention. If we get stopped we're fucked and I'll make sure Mike knows it was your fault.'

A few minutes later, a cluster of tower blocks appeared just off the main road. 'Slow down. We're turning off in a minute,' Curtis said, simultaneously dialling a number on his mobile.

Ray heard him say to whoever answered: 'We'll be there in two minutes. Is everything clear?' The reply was inaudible but Curtis then simply said: 'Right' and hung up.

'Take the next left and then turn right behind the first block of flats,' he ordered.

Ray found himself descending into an area of lock-up garages between two tower blocks with open pedestrian areas forming the garage roofs. At first sight it didn't strike him as a good place to carry out a drugs deal but then he realised there were no pedestrians in the open spaces; there was no CCTV, which he assumed would be a given in such an area and there was not another soul to be seen in or around the garages.

'Stop here,' Curtis suddenly barked. 'Wait in the van.'

He picked up one of the parcels, got out and walked forwards from the van. As he did so, one the garage doors on the left opened and two men appeared. Curtis handed over the package and turned back towards the van.

As he got back in, Ray said: 'I would've thought they would want to check the consignment.'

Curtis eyed him quizzically, then replied: 'There's no need. They're our men. They know what they've got.'

'So how does that work then?'

'You don't need to know that. Not yet anyway.'

The three remaining drops followed a very similar pattern, although one was done at a small unit in an anonymous industrial estate and one was done on a public car park. But each time there was no conversation between Curtis and the collectors and each time no attempt was made to check the contents of the package. As far as Ray could see, no money changed hands either.

After the last one Curtis climbed back into the van with the words: 'OK, that's it. Take us home.'

It took around two hours to drive back to Colchester, which passed mostly in silence, despite Ray's attempts at making small-talk. Curtis's taciturnity did, however, give him a chance to think about his situation and he decided it was time to contact his go-between, Jan. He could ring her easily enough, but then it occurred to him he wanted more than that.

He wanted to see her.

***

Jan was in the pub before him. She ordered herself a bottle of trendy Italian beer and chose a corner seat, from which she could see the length of the bar, the front door and another door to the left of the bar which led to the toilets. She had been there no more than five minutes, pretending to be busy with her mobile, when Ray arrived.

He spotted her straight away and sat down beside her. He pulled her close with his right arm and whispered in her ear: 'Kiss me.' Without hesitation she lifted her head and he felt the warm moistness of her mouth on his. For a fraction of second her lips parted but Ray drew back. 'What can I get you?' he asked. If he had been more in tune with her, he would have noticed the look of mild disappointment that crossed her face as she asked for another bottle of the Italian beer.

When he returned from the bar he sat down very close to her, so close their thighs rubbed together. She made no attempt to move away. Instead, she asked: 'What was all that about? Asking for a kiss?'

'You're supposed to be my girlfriend, don't forget,' he replied. 'I just wanted to make it look good. Just in case anybody was watching.'

'Yeah, but there's only six other people in here, including the barman.'

'All the more reason to make it look like we're together,' he said. 'Anyway, I've spent the day with a couple of proper thugs and I fancied a bit of TLC.'

Jan seemed to ignore his plea for Tender Loving Care. 'So, you're in then?'

'Yes, I'm in,' said Ray. 'And I have to say it was remarkably easy, although I can tell they don't quite trust me a hundred per cent yet. But you need to let Copeland and Wilpshire know.

'You also need to tell them that I was the driver today on what I suspect was a drugs supply run into North London. It's nothing for them to get excited about just yet — it was relatively small scale — but I think I'm getting a handle on the kind of stuff Pilling will be expecting me to do. If I play my cards right I just know it's going to get bigger.

'I've been given a guided tour of the depot but I have a feeling I was only shown what they wanted me to see, although I did see a trailer that was having some work done in it internally but I don't know what it was. And there's another big shed that Pilling appears to keep for his personal use. I was told he keeps a couple of classic cars in there but I need to get in and see for myself.'

They spent the next hour drinking more beer, idly chatting and laughing, the way lovers do. Finally Ray looked at his watch and said: 'I really need to be going. The landlady at the B and B's a bit of a harridan. I need to find a place of my own pretty soon or she's going to drive me mad.'

Jan linked her arm through his. 'I've got a lovely big flat, plenty big enough for two' she said softly, yet amazed at hearing herself say it. 'You don't have to go back to the B and B.'

Ray looked into her big brown eyes and saw that she meant it.

'Jan, we both know that I do,' he said. 'And we both know why I do.'

CHAPTER 7

At 16 Rosie was officially too young to get into the club. But a bit of make-up, the right clothes and a smattering of confidence worked wonders. She and her friend Zoe breezed in, even though a notice above the pay desk said: "Strictly Over 21s Only." The doormen hadn't even given them a second look.

Inside, no amount of black paint or fancy lighting could disguise the club's origins. It had been a factory and still looked like one — a large open space with metal columns supporting a roof maybe 40 feet above. At one end a bar ran the full width of the room and in one corner was a cluster of beanbags. A few more tables with small, plastic armchairs completed the gesture to comfort.

The other end of the room featured a stage, surrounded by flashing lights and whirling lasers, on which a DJ sat at a console, manipulating the controls of a sound system that could produce more noise than a jumbo jet at take-off.

The centre of the room was one massive dance floor and right now it was packed with young people enjoying themselves. The sound pulsing from the club's giant tower speakers made conversation impossible. The spinning, flashing, dazzling lights were disorientating. There was only thing to do. Dance. And every weekend hundreds of people came from miles around to do just that.

Rosie and Zoe picked their way through the throng, heading for the bar. Zoe, who had turned 18 only a few weeks before, put her mouth to her friend's ear.

'What do you want to drink?'

'A Coke. I'll just have a Coke please,' said Rosie, intimidated by the size of the place and the throbbing noise which seemed to make the very air she breathed move.

Even though the bar was busy there were plenty of staff on duty so it didn't take long for Zoe to catch the eye of a young man wearing a badge that said his name was Josh and that he was the assistant bar manager.

'Two vodka and cokes please,' she said. And then: 'Actually, make them large ones.'

She handed Rosie one of the big glasses. 'We'll have a dance in a minute. Let's finish these first.'

Rosie took a sip and screwed up her face. 'Ugh. It tastes funny,' she shouted at her friend.

'Yeah, sorry. It's that stuff out of a mixer,' replied Zoe. 'I've got the same. Try mine.'

Rosie accepted Zoe's explanation and carried on drinking the concoction in her hand. Five minutes later, both girls had drained their glasses and were on the dance floor.

Half an hour seemed to pass in seconds as the pair danced together in the heated crush oblivious to everything and everyone around them. But unknown to either of them, someone had been very aware of them. And suddenly he was at Zoe's side. He was about 24 or 25, average height and build, but Zoe would remember his startling green eyes which gave him the appearance of a cat. He was dressed in a stylish but well-cut light grey suit and his mop of black hair had been carefully fashioned to give it a dishevelled look. He whispered something in Zoe's ear and when she looked at him blankly, he smiled and nodded, as if in reassurance.

'Rosie, go and wait for me by the bar,' she told her friend. 'I'll be back in a few minutes.'

Puzzled but with no other person to turn to, Rosie did as she was told.

True to her word, Zoe was back in a little over five minutes and found Rosie sitting at one of the small tables. She slid into a chair and taking care that only Rosie could see what she was holding, opened her right hand.

'Look what I've got,' she said proudly. 'This should make sure the night will take off.'

Rosie stared at the four green pills, each of which had a crown logo stamped on it, nestling in her friend's palm.

'What is it?' she asked.

'It's Ecstasy,' replied Zoe. 'That bloke just sold them to me for five pounds each. That's a bargain price.'

'But Zoe, they're drugs,' said Rosie, a note of horror in her voice.

'Not really. They just make you feel good and help you dance all night. Here, try one.'

'I'm not sure I should. I mean, I've never taken anything like that before.'

'Go on, don't be a softy. I've taken Ecstasy loads of time. You'll love it. Hang on and I'll get us some more drinks to wash them down.'

Zoe returned from the bar with two more large vodka and cokes. As she sat down, she pressed one of the green pills into Rosie's hands. 'Right, here we go. One, two, three and down the hatch,' she said, swallowing a pill and taking a slug of vodka at the same time.

Rosie, still not entirely convinced by Zoe's bravado, did the same.

'How long will it take to work?' she asked.

'It depends. Twenty minutes or so. You'll know when it happens because you'll feel great and you'll just want to dance.'

The pair of them lingered over their drinks, waiting for the drug to take effect. After half an hour Rosie declared: 'I don't feel any different. Do you?'

'Yeah, I'm starting to buzz,' said Zoe. 'I feel fantastic. The lights are just brilliant. Really, really bright.'

It was a lie. And the consequences of that lie would live with Zoe forever.

'Well, it's not working for me. Give me another,' said Rosie.

Without a second thought Zoe did as she was bidden, completely unaware that what she had bought — and what she was now about to give her friend an overdose of — was not Ecstasy but the far deadlier PMA, para-Methoxyamphetamine. Instead of inducing a feeling of euphoria, PMA has the calming, sedative effects of an antidepressant. In the amounts that had now entered Rosie's body, it has serious side effects which are accelerated by alcohol.

Having swallowed the second tablet, Rosie dragged Zoe back onto the dance floor, where she spent the first 10 minutes pretending that the tablet she believed to be Ecstasy was taking effect. Very soon, she began to feel hot, a feeling that went to extremely hot and then uncomfortably hot as the PMA triggered a dramatic rise in her core body temperature.

As her temperature approached 40°C she began to experience difficulty in breathing and a feeling of nausea crept over her. She knew she was about to be sick but in her mind she blamed the vodka. Without a word to Zoe, she clamped her hand over her mouth and made a run for the toilet. She just made it, falling to her knees in a cubicle a split second before the entire contents of her stomach voided themselves into the bowl. She felt her heart begin to beat a frightening, irregular pattern. It felt like it was trying to hammer its way out of her chest.

She was still on her knees, retching, when she heard Zoe's voice. 'Rosie, Rosie. Are you OK? What's the matter?'

Rosie was unable to answer but instead managed to wave her right hand in the air. As she did so, the first convulsion struck. Her whole body began to shake and she banged her chin on the toilet rim, opening up a clean gash that bled profusely.

Somewhere in the distance she heard Zoe scream: 'Rosie, Rosie. Help me somebody. Please help me.' Then it went dark.

The arrival of an ambulance a few minutes later put a stop to the revelry going on in the club as all the main lights went on and the music was silenced. In the toilet, the two female paramedics were rapidly assessing the situation. One of them knelt by the now-still Rosie. 'Hello, can you hear me? Can you hear me?' Getting no response she called to no one and everyone: 'What's her name? Does anybody know her name?'

'Rosie. She's called Rosie,' Zoe volunteered.

'Has she taken anything?' asked the second paramedic as her kneeling colleague put her ear to Rosie's mouth to determine whether she was still breathing. Zoe looked blank. 'Tell me,' the raised voice demanded. 'What has she taken?'

Left with no choice, Zoe dug in her purse and held out the green tablet with the crown logo. 'She's had two of these,' she said. 'It's Ecstasy.'

The paramedic's eyes opened wide. 'No it's not,' she said, then turning to her colleague added: 'She's taken PMA. Two tabs of Green Rolex. We need to get her to A&E urgently.'

Suddenly everything happened in a blur and the next thing Zoe was aware of was sitting in the back of an ambulance as a paramedic worked to keep Rosie stabilised against a background of a wailing siren and crackled radio messages. She followed meekly as the paramedics rushed Rosie into the A&E department where a crash team was already waiting.

One of the paramedics was briefing a doctor. 'This is Rosie. She's 16 years-old. Suspected drug overdose. She's taken two tablets of these,' handing the doctor the one remaining Green Rolex tablet in a plastic bag. 'We believe it's PMA. She's remained unconscious and has had two convulsions, one of them in the ambulance. She's tachycardic and hyperthermic. Her temperature is 40.3°C and her blood pressure is 170 over 110. She also has a laceration to her chin.'

'Right people,' the doctor said loudly, 'we need to get to work on this one straight away. We'll start with her temperature. I need a litre of cooled saline immediately.'

The medical team worked tirelessly to help the now comatose Rosie. The cooled saline was given intravenously to try to bring her core body temperature down to manageable levels. Another IV drip fed sodium nitroprusside into her blood stream to bring down her dangerously high blood pressure and she was injected with a benzodiazepine to control her convulsions.

The battle went on for more than an hour but the Green Rolex proved to be an indefatigable foe. Induced by the reaction her body had had to the drug, Rosie's major organs began to fail one by one until finally her heart stopped beating. Increasingly strong jolts from the defibrillator failed to restart it and so it was that just after two o'clock in the morning, the A&E consultant said to his team: 'There's no point in continuing. She's dead. Does everyone agree?' Around the emergency table there were sad grunts and nods of assent.

As the team moved away to await the next fight for life, a solitary nurse began the task of disassembling the paraphernalia of the struggle.

No one would ever suspect that the drug that killed Rosie was delivered into the dealer network by a serving police officer working undercover for the National Crime Agency.

CHAPTER 8

Ray did three more drug drops with George Curtis sitting alongside him before he was trusted enough to be allowed out on his own. And when he was, Pilling ran him ragged. One day he did drops in Brighton, Portsmouth, Southampton and Aldershot; the next day he went to Birmingham, Manchester and Liverpool; on the third day he went to Swindon, Bath and Bristol.

By the time Friday came around he felt like his eyeballs had been peeled. He was looking forward to a relaxing weekend doing nothing, maybe spending a bit of no-pressure time with Jan while he came to terms with what he was now involved in. He was effectively a criminal, heavily involved in the supply of illegal drugs and if he got caught there would be no way out. The NCA would deny all knowledge of him. He would be treated no differently to anyone else caught dealing. He would be charged, probably remanded in custody and then brought before a court to face the judgment of his peers, potentially looking at a life sentence.

But before he got the chance to think too deeply about the position he was in, Pilling sent for him. It was almost five o'clock — knocking off time for most of the Pilling Transport employees. 'Welbourne I've got a very special job for you tomorrow,' said Pilling as Ray entered his office. 'There's an urgent drop come up but it's a bit different to what you've been doing.'

'Different how?' asked Ray.

'It's a cash-in-hand job. And I'm trusting you to bring the money back here and put it in the safe.'

'How much cash?'

'Not that you need to know, but it's thirty grand,' replied Pilling, staring icily into Ray's eyes. 'I know that might be a lot to you but don't even think about trying to cheat me. If you do, I'll find you and believe me, you won't like the result.'

'It had never crossed my mind boss,' said Ray. 'I was just curious. So what do I have to do?'

'You know Leicester Forest services on the M1? You need to be there for 10.30. Stay in the van and wait until you are approached. There should be two of them and they will know your name. They will give you cash. Check it before you hand over the goods. When you're happy, open the van and let them take away the package.'

'What's in it?' Ray asked.

'You don't need to know that. Just make sure the money's right and that they take the package. Then bring the money back here,' said Pilling. He opened a drawer and threw a set of keys across the desk to Ray.

'These are the keys for the main gates, the office and the garage. The safe is built into the floor under Summer's desk. It will be empty and it won't be locked. Put the money inside and give the combination a spin. Then lock up, put the van back in the garage and take the keys home with you. Any questions?'

'Just one, where will I find the package I'm delivering?'

'Don't worry about that, it will be in the back of the van when you get here.'

'OK boss, leave it me. See you on Monday,' said Ray, clutching the keys tightly as if they were made of precious metal because, in his eyes, that's exactly what there were — they were worth their weight in gold.

***

The following morning Ray was pulling out of the depot gates at a few minutes after seven o'clock, leaving himself time for the almost three hour journey to Leicester Forest East services. He had checked to make sure the package was on board and discovered there were two parcels, each wrapped in bubbled plastic and sealed with gaffer tape like all the others he had delivered, but these two were much heavier and he guessed they were not drugs. Even if he had known what was inside the packages there was nothing he could it about it. He was committed now. The delivery had to be made.

The smaller of the parcels contained 12 boxes of 9mm hollow point ammunition, with 100 rounds in each box. The other box contained two MAC10 submachine guns with sound suppressors; two Glock 17 semi-automatic pistols; two of the very latest Sig Sauer P320 semi-automatic pistols carrying 9mm slides and barrels and two Russian made Baikal pistols. The Baikals were originally made to fire 8mm gas cartridges for crowd control but because they were made from solid steel, they were easy to convert to fire 9mm bullets. They were also relatively cheap compared to the other weapons in the consignment; they were accurate and had a reputation for being indestructible, all of which made them extremely popular in the criminal community.

Ray arrived at the service area just after 10am and reversed into a parking space on the very edge of the car park, right up against the motorway fence. He toyed with the idea of getting a coffee but decided against it — he might not know what he was carrying but he did know it was worth £30,000 — so he just sat and waited.

Just before 10.30am he watched a black Mercedes people carrier with blacked out windows and displaying Northern Ireland registration plates pull on to the car park. It did a complete circuit before coming to a halt in a parking space directly facing him. Ray could see two men inside, both wearing sunglasses despite the fact that the day was overcast. The driver appeared to share the same bull-headed build as George Curtis while the passenger would have passed unnoticed in any crowd. He was average height, average build and dressed in averagely casual clothes which, Ray noticed, carried no designer logos, no bright colours, nothing that would attract a second glance.

Mr Average pulled a piece of paper from his pocket and checked something before the pair strode over to Ray's van and stood at the driver's door. Ray lowered the window.

'You Ray Welbourne?' asked Mr Average.

'Yeah.'

'You got something for us.' It was a statement rather than a question and the accent was definitely not Northern Irish.

'Yeah, if you've got the cash.'

'We have. Come over to our van and count it.'

'No thanks,' replied Ray. 'Bring it over and I'll count it here.'

Mr Average nodded to the bull-head who opened his leather jacket and produced a bulging, brown A3 envelope which he passed to Ray.

The envelope was unsealed. Ray tipped the contents onto the passenger seat and out tumbled bundles of brand new £50 notes. A quick count revealed 15 of them, each one therefore worth £2,000. He picked up the first bundle and licked his right index finger.

'This might take a while,' he told Mr Average. 'Do you want to get a coffee or something while I count it?'

'No. We'll just wait here. Not that we don't trust you or anything.'

It took Ray almost an hour to count the notes and when he was satisfied he wound the window down and said to Mr Average: 'OK, I'm happy. I'll open the back for you.'

Mr Average picked up the smaller of the packages, leaving bull-head with the biggest and heaviest. 'Pleasure doing business with you, my friend,' was his parting shot. Even before they had loaded the packages into their people carrier, Ray was on his way back to Essex.

He arrived at the Pilling depot a little after three in the afternoon and, as he anticipated, the place was deserted. He unlocked the office and took the envelope full of cash inside. It took him a couple of minutes to find the drop safe because it was concealed from view by a floor tile, of which there half a dozen under Summer's desk. He dropped the money inside, spun the combination lock and replaced the floor tile.

Then he unlocked the garage, drove the Transit inside and closed the door from the inside. This was the moment he had been waiting for; his first chance to have a close look around; his first chance to explore the secrets of Pilling Transport.

The trailer from which he had heard the banging and clattering was still there but, peering inside, he could see nothing out of the ordinary. He climbed inside, tapping the sides and the bulkhead in the hope that a hidden compartment might reveal itself. He examined the floor for a hidden recess but there was nothing. A few crumbs of sawdust were the only confirmation that he had not imagined what he had heard. Just to be sure he took a photograph with his phone camera: somebody else could interpret it.

He moved through the open internal door into the warehouse and made his way to the shelving stack in the centre. Even though he had spent the best part of two weeks delivering whatever had been stored there — and by now he was sure it was a profitable mix of drugs — the shelves were full once again. The supply, wherever it came from, was constant and consistent.

He took more photographs before checking to see if there was any variation in the weight and size of the store packages. Most of them seemed identical, probably pre-packed consignments which had a combined street value running into millions of pounds. Others were bulkier, bigger, heavier. For no other reason than the notion seemed to fit, Ray decided that these heavier packages in all likelihood contained firearms which had no doubt been broken down into their component parts to make discovery by X-ray, should that possibility arise, more difficult.

His attention then turned to the hatch in the floor, the only one that was clean and showed signs of being opened. It was unlocked and opened with a simple twist fastener. As soon as he began to lift the lid he knew what was inside. The smell was unmistakable. Even the rawest recruit would have no difficulty in identifying it. It was mix of composting grass cuttings and wet wood chippings; an earthy kind of smell. Cannabis.

After the smell came the heat from the arc lights producing the 2,000 Watts of power that cannabis needs for 12 hours a day during the three months it takes to crop. Ray's immediate thought was that surely, this amount of heat would have been spotted by the police helicopter's heat-seeking camera. But, then again, the police would have to have been looking for it to find it. And once inside, he realised the "roof" of the cannabis farm was covered in thick insulation, which would dramatically reduce the amount of heat escaping.

The area was probably 100 metres long and 30 metres wide. Ducting in the ceiling carried gas, water and electricity, he assumed, but the whole of the floor space was taken up by cannabis plants and their life-giving lights. From the smell they were giving off, Ray guessed the plants were almost ready for harvesting. He decided not to investigate further; he'd seen all he needed to, so he took more pictures and got out, taking care to replace the hatch exactly as he had found it.

Before he left the depot, he searched the internet via his mobile phone and found a local security specialist that would cut keys while he waited. He called to check the shop was open and an hour later he emerged with a duplicate set of keys in his hand.

Back in his B&B room he put the duplicates in a drawer. Then he copied the photographs from his phone to his laptop and then from his laptop to a flash drive, which he concealed in a sock inside his holdall before deleting all the images from both devices.

He hadn't got much, except the picture of the cannabis farm. The other images could have been anything and were not, of themselves, evidence.

As yet, he had nothing to link the Pilling Transport depot with The Hydra and he had not yet been able to search for evidence that might show which judges, senior police officers and Whitehall mandarins the organisation had in its pocket. And he still had to get into the big shed that Curtis had described as being Mike's.

Ray put these thoughts to the back of his mind and glanced at his watch. Just after five o'clock. He could spend an hour or two trawling the internet for a suitable flat in the area, then maybe go for a pint at the local pub and have an early night with his book. At all costs, he wanted to avoid sitting in the B&B's communal lounge watching mindless television and being evasive of his fellow guests.

Or he could ring Jan and spend a relaxing evening in her company over a meal and a few drinks. She might even know of a flat that would suit his purposes. It occurred to him that not only was she the nearest thing he had to a friend there and then, he actually enjoyed being with her. She made him laugh — and laughs had been few and far between lately.

From the second she answered her phone Ray knew he had made a mistake. She was obviously in a bar somewhere. He could hear the clamour of lots of people in the background. He could hear the sound of chinking glass and the distant hum of music. 'Sorry Ray, I'm already out with someone,' she replied to his suggestion that they meet, quickly adding: 'I'm with a couple of girls from the flats. We're going for a curry in a minute and then we're going to the cinema. I'd say come with us but I don't think it's your kind of film.'

His evening was planned for him.

***

The following morning he was late down to breakfast, just making it before the 9.30am cut-off time. The bonus was that his three fellow guests had already eaten and left.

'Ah, good morning Mr Welbourne. I thought you weren't going to join us this morning.' The hint of sarcasm in his landlady's voice irritated him slightly.

'Sorry Mrs Clayton I slept like a log. I've had a busy week and it must have caught up on me.'

'Don't worry, somebody's got to be last. Full English? Tea and toast?'

She returned a few minutes later with a rack of cold toast and a stainless steel teapot that wouldn't hold enough to fill a decent sized mug and sat down in the chair facing him.

'Mr Welbourne, you know you said you were looking for a place to live locally? Well, I think I might be able to help you. My niece — my sister's youngest actually — well, she works in town for one of the big estate agents.'

Ray's face feigned interest while his brain was saying '*For God's sake get on with it woman.*'

'And she's told me that they've got a flat on their books that might suit. It's in a block near the hospital. It's only got one bedroom, but the thing is, it's furnished and I think the price might suit you too. She says it's £750 a month.'

Ray pondered for a few seconds. He really had to get a place of his own; he couldn't function living in a B&B — the risk of exposure was too high. It was worth a look.

'That's very kind of you Mrs Clayton,' he said. 'Can your niece organise a viewing for me? I should be able to make any evening this week.

'Well, she's working today if you're not doing anything special. They work all hours these days you know.' She didn't specify who "they" were but Ray assumed she was referring to estate agents.

'Er, no. Well, nothing I can't change. Any time today would be good.'

Before he had finished breakfast, Mrs Clayton had organised his viewing and arranged for her niece to meet him.

He found the address easily enough and parked the 10 year-old BMW, provided by the NCA, outside what he assumed was the main entrance. The car ran perfectly well although it had seen better days. The paint work had lost its shine, the alloy wheels were pitted and scraped and there were a couple of dents and noticeable scratches on the body work. But it fitted his back-story and wasn't going to get him noticed. What Ray did not know was that fastened to the chassis, close to the near-side rear wheel was a tracking device, fitted by the NCA before they handed it over.

He had just locked the car when a small red Nissan Micra pulled up on the opposite side of the street and a young woman emerged. She was in her early 20s, plump, plain and had made no attempt to improve things with make-up and smart clothes. At first Ray dismissed her as a local resident but she walked confidently towards him.

'Are you Mr Welbourne? I'm Julie. Julie Fisher. From the estate agents.' The last sentence had an upward inflection that made it sound like a question.

'Yes. Yes I am,' he replied, taking her out-stretched hand.

As if she had read his mind, Julie quickly added: 'Forgive the state of me. I don't normally dress like this for work. It's just that it's Sunday and we don't normally do viewings on a Sunday but my aunt said today was the only day you could do it.'

She's in quite a rush to get rid of me then, thought Ray.

Less than an hour later, he was in the estate agent's office where he used a credit card to pay a month's rent in advance as a deposit, signed a lease that could be terminated by one month's notice in writing and completed a direct debit mandate drawn on a bank in Cambridge, his home town. He emerged carrying a copy of the lease and the keys to his new home.

Mrs Clayton made unconvincing noises about how sad she was to see him go, but wished him well in his new flat. And then closed the door behind him before he'd got to the gate.

He rang Jan to give her the news, dropped his solitary suitcase at the flat then headed off to a local superstore where he bought two pillows, a double duvet, two duvet covers, sheets and towels. By the time he got back, Jan was waiting for him with a bottle of champagne and two glasses.

'Well, I am supposed to be your girlfriend,' she said by way of explanation. 'So I thought we should toast the occasion properly.'

After the first glass, she offered to make his bed and set about unwrapping all the things he had bought. Ray leaned on the door jamb, a second glass of bubbly in his hand, watching her at work. It struck him how lithe and supple she was as she moved around the bed, something he had never noticed about her before. Her shoulder-length auburn hair fell across her face as she bent here, tucked there. He felt a stirring inside, a stirring he rapidly attributed to champagne-fuelled lust that was unprofessional, not to mention downright stupid.

He left her to her work and went back into the living room.

When the bed had been made to her satisfaction and the champagne had been drained, they headed out in search of somewhere to eat and found a Thai restaurant a few streets away. A bottle of dry white washed down the food, after which they wandered into a pub, from which the sound of live music was blasting. Afterwards, he knew he should have resisted Jan's suggestion of a nightcap at his new place. But he didn't.

He wouldn't fully remember going to bed but when his mobile phone alarm shocked him back to life just before seven o'clock the following morning, he realised he was alone. And had been all night.

CHAPTER 9

For a Monday morning, Mike Pilling was in a remarkably good mood. Even in the short time he had worked there, Ray had realised that Monday mornings were a potentially volatile time, depending on how many drugs — and in what combinations — Pilling had ingested over the weekend. But this morning his face was cracked by a tight smile when he rolled into the office just before nine o'clock. It was the first time Ray had ever seen him sporting anything other than a dour expression but, given the gauntness of his prematurely aged face, the smile succeeded only in making him look even more like a death's head.

For once he didn't bark at Summer or sneer at Ray. 'Good morning all,' he said. 'Everybody had a good weekend?'

'Looks like you have,' replied Summer, but Pilling ignored her.

'When you've finished your tea, will you come into the office Ray?'

Ray had no idea what to expect, but there was no malice in his voice so he drained his mug and wandered in.

'I got a phone call from Vic on Saturday night. He's the guy you took the delivery to,' Pilling began. 'He called me to say how impressed he was by the way you handled yourself. He said you didn't take any chances; that you wouldn't let the consignment go until you'd counted the money. I like that too. Vic's one of our biggest clients so if he's happy, I'm happy. I thought you might like to know. Well done.'

'Thanks Boss,' Ray said. 'Good to know that I'm doing OK.'

'You're doing more than OK. In fact, I think we might put your HGV skills to the test in a few days. How do you fancy a run to the Continent?'

'Yeah, I'll give that a whirl. Where to exactly?'

'Not far. Bonn in Germany.'

'Great. When do I leave?'

'I'm waiting on confirmation of the loads, but probably tomorrow,' Pilling replied. 'I'll let you know.'

***

It was late on Monday afternoon, after Ray had returned from yet another drugs run, that Pilling called him into the office. 'The Germany job's on for tomorrow,' he told Ray. 'You need to drive to Ipswich: this is the address.' He flicked a yellow Post-It note across the desk. 'You'll be picking up a load of second hand furniture — there's big market in British antique furniture in Germany. The delivery address will be on the consignment note you'll be given and you're booked on the overnight ferry from Harwich to the Hook of Holland. For the return leg, you'll be carrying a load of oriental rugs and carpets but they need to be taken to a place called Vlissingen. It's on the coast North West of Antwerp. You're booked on the overnight ferry back to Harwich from the Hook on Thursday. You'll be empty but it can't be helped. Any questions?'

'Have I got a mate or am I on my own?' Ray asked.

'You're on your own. I'm trusting you with this one,' Pilling replied. 'Do what you've been told; don't ask questions; don't fuck it up and you'll be all right. You've got the depot keys so just bring the truck back here on Saturday and I'll see you next week.'

***

The ferry nosed its way into the Hook of Holland ferry port just after six o'clock in the morning on what promised to be a bright, sunny day. But Ray felt anything but bright and sunny. Even though the crossing had only taken a little over six hours, he had spent most of it wide awake thanks to the snoring, belching and farting of his fellow travellers who, like him, had decided to sleep in the main lounge.

As he drove the 40-tonne truck from the bowels of the ferry onto the quayside, it occurred to him that he hadn't slept for almost 24 hours and was probably in no fit state to drive anything — let alone a vehicle this big. The queue to leave the port was flowing freely as the Dutch Customs officers took very little interest in the cars, vans and trucks that were rolling into their country.

His on-board sat-nav system guided him successfully through the unremarkable town that was the Hook — actually a district of the city of Rotterdam — and out towards a motorway designated A59. The route took Ray south east towards Eindhoven, then east towards Cologne before turning south heading for Bonn. His tiredness and the fact that he wasn't used to the HGV meant he kept his speed low, so it took more than four hours to cover the 145 miles from the port to his destination in the district of Meindorf on the north side of the River Rhine and well away from the historic centre of Bonn.

When he arrived at the medium sized industrial unit, he was unsurprised that the gatekeeper spoke perfect English, directing him to where his vehicle would be unloaded before adding it would be at least an hour until men would be available for the task. Sensing the disappointment in Ray's eyes, he added there was a caravan a couple of hundred metres up the road where he could get excellent coffee and something to eat.

Half an hour later, he was back in the truck. The gatekeeper had been right about the coffee; it was excellent, but the food left a little to be desired. He was listening to an audio-book CD of Joseph Conrad's "Typhoon" when there was a knock on the window and he found himself staring into the eyes of a huge Dutchman who could have come directly from Hell's Angels casting. The man stood well over six feet tall and judging by the size of his stomach, Ray guessed he weighed in excess of 20 stones. His shoulder length black hair was streaked with grey and tied back with a dirty bandana. A stained white tee shirt and a heavily studded, sleeveless black leather jerkin stretched around him. Both arms were covered in tattoos. Ray noticed that a dotted line was tattooed around his neck with the words "Cut Here" in English, just below his Adam's apple.

'We're just going to start unloading,' he said, betraying only a slight Dutch accent as Ray lowered the window. 'It should take us about an hour but it's going to be tonight before we can load your return cargo.'

'Tonight? What time tonight?' This was a prospect Ray had not foreseen.

'Just tonight,' replied the man. 'Don't leave the truck. I'll knock when we're ready to start.'

Ray followed him to the back of the vehicle where he found another four men, all of whom were identical to the first. He unlocked the trailer doors and then decided it was time to catch upon his sleep. He climbed back into the cab, locked the door behind him and crawled into the bunk behind the driver's seat. Sleep overtook him almost immediately. There he remained, warm and comfortable, oblivious to his surroundings, until a banging on the door and an insistent voice shouting 'Driver; Driver' awakened him with a shock. He glanced at his watch. Six-thirty. He had been asleep for more than three hours.

Outside he found the Number One Hell's Angel and his four clones. 'Unlock the back; we're ready to load your cargo.'

'OK. Rugs and carpets isn't it?' Ray asked, trying to sound casual. He spotted a knowing glance pass between the five men facing him.

'Yes. That's it. Rugs and carpets,' replied Number One.

'For delivery to Vlissingen.'

'Yes. Vlissingen.'

'I don't have the address though.'

'You will have by the time you leave here. Now get back in and close the curtains. I'll knock again when we've finished loading.'

Ray did as he was told. Inside the cab he put the Joseph Conrad audio book back on and lay down on his bunk. From behind his head he could hear the men moving about in the trailer, followed by the sound of what he thought was drilling. He had no idea what was happening and he could think of no good reason why they should be drilling anything, but from Number One's demeanour, he decided it would wise not to ask.

Ten minutes later, he had dozed off but was awakened by the sound of several muffled voices, speaking a language he could not recognise. They were replaced by scraping noises and the sound of renewed drilling. When the drilling ended, he could hear things being dragged into the trailer and a brief argument began in Dutch. Then all was quiet.

Ray was briefly lost in the voice of the narrator reading "Typhoon" when a demanding banging on the driver's door indicated that the loading was complete. Leaving the curtain closed, Ray opened the door and climbed out. Number One, menacing simply because of his size, was standing there with a young girl. Ray guessed she was in her late teens or early twenties, but the word that went through his mind at first sight was "Waif."

She was thin — painfully so — and surrounded by an aura of wretchedness. The clothes she wore were threadbare. Her short, dark hair was dishevelled, the pale skin of her face streaked by tears and she carried the care-worn expression that is peculiar to the neglected and the unloved. Her eyes, though big and round, were dulled and radiated about as much light as two pit shafts. She carried a supermarket plastic bag, printed in a language that Ray did not recognise, that contained what few possessions she had.

'Who's this?' asked Ray.

'She's coming with you to Vlissingen,' the Number One replied.

'No one said anything about passengers,' said Ray. 'What do I do with her?'

The girl's terrified eyes swivelled between the two men.

'Leave her with the people who unload the truck.'

'And then what?'

'Fuck off back to England.' A brown A5 envelope was thrust at Ray. 'The address you're going to is in there. And there's a consignment note confirming the load, where it's come from and where you're taking it. Just in case...'

He picked the girl up under one arm as if she was matchwood, carried her to the passenger door and heaved her into the cab then, without saying another word he walked off into the warehouse behind the truck.

The first twenty minutes of the journey were broken only by the whimpering coming from Ray's passenger, who sat half turned towards the window with her head resting on the glass. Eventually, he asked: 'Do you speak English?' but the question went unanswered. Not sure whether it was because the girl did not understand or whether she simply did not want to talk to him, he tried another tack.

'What's your name?' he asked.

This time the whimpering stopped and she turned in the seat so that she was now facing the front instead of looking through the side window, but a move that still made eye contact impossible.

'What's your name?' Ray repeated. 'What should I call you?'

She glanced at him, as if unsure of what he was saying. And then: 'Anna. My name is Anna.'

'Well, pleased to meet you Anna,' he said. 'My name's Ray.'

He heard her repeat 'Ray' and then she fell silent again.

'Tell me Anna, how old are you?'

There was a few seconds hesitation. 'I am nineteen. Nineteen years old.'

'And where are you from?'

Again a hesitation while she struggled to translate his words in her head. 'I from Albania. Things very bad there. No money, no jobs. Very bad. I get away.'

'And where are you going?' Ray asked.

'I go England. I have good job there.'

Ray immediately sensed he had been conned. The Hell's Angel had simply dumped this pathetic creature on him and expected him to sort it out.

'Hang on, I can't take you to England. I don't know you. I don't know anything about you.'

Anna's face creased in tears. 'Pleess. I desperate. I do anything. Anything. You want make fuck? I let. But I need go Vlissingen. Then go England. Pleess.'

The hard-bitten copper in him suddenly melted as he realised that this 19 year-old bag of bones was willing to give her body to him — willing to give it to anybody she thought could help her — because she wanted to flee her old life and was so desperate she would do anything to achieve her goal.

'Why do you need to go Vlissingen? There are no ships sailing to England from there.'

'I go Vlissingen catch boat,' she answered. 'Eight of us all go England. We pay plenty money in Albania.'

'Eight of you? Where are the others then?' he asked.

'In trailer. Hidden. There was no room for me.'

And now he knew he had been conned. Not only by the Hell's Angel but by Mike Pilling and everyone who had known anything about his journey. He felt the fury building inside him and struggled hard to remind himself that this is what he was here to do. To gather the information that would lead to the evidence that in turn would lead to the downfall of the Hydra. He had to keep his feelings bottled up.

'You said you had a job in England,' he said calmly. 'What is it you are going to do?'

'I have good job in show business,' she answered. 'In night club. Maybe singer. I don't know.'

Yeah? I bet it's not the kind of show business you're thinking of, the cynic in him said. 'That should be exciting,' the nice guy in him said out loud. 'Have you done any singing before?'

'I sing in church choir when I very small,' she said. 'But not really proper singing.'

Ray managed a rueful smile, knowing that Anna and her friends would never achieve their dreams. Pole dancers, strippers at best but, more likely, they would end up in seedy brothels, earning a fortune for their unseen masters while being fed a constant diet of Class A drugs to keep them compliant.

'Don't forget me when you're rich and famous,' he said.

She did not reply and the silence fell upon them again until, an hour later, after skirting around the port of Antwerp, they turned left and soon passed a signpost that said: "Vlissingen. 50km."

Anna began to relax. She was almost there. Her dreams were almost fulfilled. It wouldn't be long before she was in England and then everything would be alright. She began to hum softly to herself, a tune that meant nothing to Ray except that, for the first time since this leg of the journey began, his passenger was behaving like a 19 year-old.

As they approached Vlissingen the sat-nav was showing him their final destination was a place called Bijleveldhaven and before long it was urging him to make a left turn on to the N254.

Anna's grasp of English was sufficient for her to realise that they were turning away from Vlissingen and she started to panic. 'No, no. We go Vlissingen. We go Vlissingen.'

Ray passed her the consignment note he had been given in Germany and showed her that it gave Bijleveldhaven as the destination. 'No. Look. It says there I have to take you to this place, Bijleveldhaven. That must be where you are getting your boat to England. I told you there are no ships to England from Vlissingen any more. I'm sure it will be alright, just you see.'

Anna looked at him quizzically. 'Promise this not trick.'

'I can't make you that promise Anna,' Ray said 'because I don't know. But it's the place I was supposed to bring you and your friends. You have to trust me.'

'You come with us?' she asked.

'No, I can't. I have to take the truck somewhere else.' He knew that if he told her he was driving back to England she would beg him to take her with him, something he simply could not afford to do. 'But you've got this far. There's not far to go now. You're nearly there.'

'You tell truth?'

'Yes Anna, I tell truth.' He didn't add: *as far as I know it.*

The cold grey streaks of dawn were cracking the sky as the truck moved slowly into the unlovely, heavily industrialised area of which Bijleveldhaven is part, the sat-nav continuing to guide him until he was confronted by a small, modern dockside warehouse standing alone and surrounded by a high wire fence. *Almost a smaller version of Pilling Transport's base*, he thought. A man appeared, unlocked the two gates, swung them open and beckoned him through. As the truck edged in, the shutter door of the warehouse began to roll up and another man signalled that he should drive in.

Ray pulled on the parking brake and switched off the engine, leaving the truck in gear. Without a word to Anna, he opened the driver's door and jumped out, almost into the arms of massively built, barrel of a man.

'Whoa! Where the fuck do you think you're going?' asked the man in an unmistakable South London accent.

'I need the loo,' said Ray. 'And I need to stretch my legs. I've been in that cab for close on four hours.

'Over there in the corner,' the man replied. 'Then get straight back here.'

When he returned Frank Chiswell, the wanted Brit who was now one of the Hydra's enforcers in Holland, was waiting for him. 'Right you. Back in the cab and stay there until I tell you different. OK?' he barked at Ray. 'And don't look out of the windows. And while I'm at it, what's that fucking girl doing in your cab?'

Ray explained she was put there in Germany, apparently because there was no room for her in the back.

'Fair enough, I'll take her with the others,' said Chiswell. 'I thought she belonged to you and I was going to tell you to make sure she stayed put too but if she's one of ours...'

Ray's heart was gripped by a feeling that could have been horror at the prospects that awaited Anna or a bitter regret that he'd told Chiswell the truth and by doing so had missed the chance — an outside one, but a chance nonetheless — to save her from her fate.

He climbed back into the cab and found Anna still sitting there. 'It's time for you to go,' he said softly. 'Good luck and may your God go with you.'

She stared at him for a full ten seconds. 'Thank you Mr Ray. You good man.' Then she leaned across and kissed him gently on the cheek. 'Goodbye.'

As she closed the cab door behind her, he felt the tears well up in his eyes. He was stricken by this young girl's courage, her passion, her self-belief. She had turned her back on everything and everybody she knew in a bid to build a new life for herself. She had a dream and she fervently believed it was about to come true.

But Ray knew differently. And now he was powerless to do anything about it.

CHAPTER 10

As he drove away he could easily identify the warehouse where he had left Anna on the opposite side of the small harbour. In the water immediately below the warehouse he could see an old clinker-built trawler — he guessed between 50 and 60 feet long — with an aft wheelhouse, deep freeboard and a blue-painted hull. A varnished nameplate was screwed to her bow, but at that distance Ray couldn't read what she was called. He also noticed that moored behind the fishing vessel was a modern cabin cruiser, slightly smaller, but with a high flying bridge that would provide the helmsman with excellent all-round visibility. Her white hull and stainless steel deck fittings gleamed in the sunlight.

It struck him that the cruiser looked out of place, even more out of place than the old trawler. She was obviously not a fishing boat, at least not a commercial one, but neither was she the posing-party boat that her sleek lines suggested. Neither Ray, nor any other casual onlooker, would ever have guessed her true purpose in a month of Sundays.

He took his time over the return journey to the Hook, stopping off for lunch at a roadside truckstop, after which he treated himself to a couple of hours snoozing. He arrived at the ferry port three hours before the scheduled sailing time and was surprised to find two other trucks already waiting in the loading area. He locked his cab and went into the terminal building in search of the ferry company's ticket desk where he splashed out £30 for a cabin. This time he was determined to get a good night's sleep.

***

At about the time Ray was driving his truck onto the ferry, two men unlocked the door to the room where Anna and her seven travelling companions had spent the day. In the darkness they took the girls, each clutching a pathetic bag of belongings, out of the warehouse, across the quay towards the blue-hulled fishing boat. No words passed between the men and the girls. It was as if the girls were programmed; as if their movements were pre-determined. They asked no questions; raised no objections. They simply followed the first man down a short gangway onto the boat's deck and gathered in a huddle.

Just forward of the wheelhouse a deck hatch had been raised and was propped open. A man's head appeared in the hatch and in English ordered the girls: 'This way.' In single file they stepped gingerly through the hatch and down a short wooden companionway. They found themselves in an open space, devoid of any natural light or creature comforts. In the centre of the bare cabin were two large piles of sugar-bag sized parcels, each individually wrapped in black plastic, the whole lot covered by transparent plastic sheeting and lashed to the cabin sole by thick canvas webbing.

Down each side of the cabin ran a continuous pipe-cot — nothing more than canvas stretched tightly over a metal frame — and towards the bow was a sea toilet set in what appeared to be a three-sided steel cage. It offered no privacy. The only light in the cabin came from four bulkhead lights fitted with red bulbs, a cruel indicator, if only the girls could recognise it, of their destiny.

Anna stared around in disbelief. 'We want go England,' she said to the man who had led them down here.

'You are,' he said.

'No. We need go England. Need big boat,' she protested.

'There's eight of you. How big a fucking boat do you want?' the man said. 'You'll be told when we get there. Now sit down and shut up. All of you.'

He hopped back on deck and closed the hatch behind him. Below, the girls heard the sound of a bolt scraping home.

A few minutes later, they heard the engines start, quickly followed by shouted instructions from above and, imperceptibly at first, the trawler began to move. In their eerily lit surroundings, the girls' excitement rose with every knot the boat's speed increased. Their new lives were now just a few hours away. Even Anna was convinced and in the red glow of the bulkhead lights, she began to hum again.

In the wheelhouse, the two crewmen guided the trawler out of the dock that was Bijleveldhaven and made a turn to the right. For almost an hour, the vessel sailed slowly past dozens of ships of all shapes and sizes, gas tankers, oil tankers, container carriers, bulk carriers, working boats big and small that all plied their business in the industrial port of Vlissingen.

As the trawler approached the breakwater at Fort Rammeken, the crew made sure she was well away from the turbulence created by the huge sluice gates that constantly drained water into the dock and she passed safely into the Westerschelde, the estuary of the Scheldt River that, to the east, led to the giant port of Antwerp.

Behind them, the crew could see the navigation lights of the cabin cruiser which had been moored behind them. It kept its distance, maintaining a matching speed, until both boats were well past the town of Vlissingen with only the open North Sea ahead of them. One of the men in the trawler checked to make sure the two boats were alone and then flashed a white light three times at the following cabin cruiser. His signal was answered by another three white flashes.

The trawler's speed was cut and she hove to. Less than a minute later the cruiser was alongside, its massive soft plastic fenders ensuring there was no impact between the two vessels, and the two crewmen stepped from the cramped, noisy, diesel-smelling wheelhouse into a world of white leather, polished teak and gleaming steel. They exchanged greetings with the two men on board the cruiser then went below in search of beer and food from the boat's groaning galley.

On the cruiser's flying bridge, one of the men flicked open an aluminium case and took from it a sophisticated radio controller; the sort of device which would have been familiar to anyone who flew a model aeroplane or sailed a model yacht. But this one could do more — much more — than simply operate basic controls.

First, using the controller, the man switched on the trawler's GPS navigation system and then programmed it with a series of waypoints — latitude and longitude co-ordinates — to which the trawler would sail on its 60-mile voyage across the North Sea. Then he activated the trawler's auto-helm system and brought the engine up to an operational level that would propel the boat forwards at a speed of 10 knots. Finally, he flicked another switch that turned on small cameras in the trawler's bow and stern. The ghostly green pictures from the cameras' image intensifiers flickered onto a small screen built into the controller, allowing him to see what was ahead of the trawler and — just as importantly given its cargo — anything that tried to approach it from behind.

The dark bulk of the trawler pulled away from the sleek cruiser on her pre-determined course which would take her south of the regular ferry route from Harwich to the Hook of Holland to a point somewhere off the Essex coast. Soon, all that the cruiser's crew could see of her were her navigation lights, bright against the starless sky.

By remotely controlling the trawler, the Hydra had removed a significant risk in the smuggling of people: the risk of capture. If the Coastguard or the Royal Navy did by any chance board the vessel, all they would find would be the human cargo and a collection of off-the-shelf electronic equipment that would be virtually untraceable. There would be no one to arrest; no one to pursue.

In the bowels of the trawler, the eight girls were unaware that they were now alone on the sea; the movement of their boat controlled remotely, their destiny in the hands of a man holding a complex guidance system on another vessel five miles behind them. And, unlike the men now on board the cruiser, they had nothing to eat and nothing to drink. They would have to live on hope and expectation.

Two hours earlier, the cargo ship MV Orion had left Rotterdam at the start of her voyage to Lagos, Nigeria. She was heading south west for the Straits of Dover, the English Channel and the Atlantic Ocean, making 15 knots, her holds full of grain. The sea was calm, visibility was good under almost total cloud cover and the off-duty watch were watching a film in the mess. Even on the bridge the atmosphere was relaxed, with no obvious problems to cause any concern.

Except the 25,000 tonne ship was on a collision course with a small blue trawler carrying eight helpless young girls.

It was the lookout on the port wing of the bridge that saw it first; just a green light, which told him he was looking at the starboard side of a vessel and a single white light, which told him the vessel was less than 50 metres long and under power.

'We've got a small vessel to port on a converging course,' he reported to the Officer of the Watch. 'It's probably a couple of kilometres away.'

'OK. Keep an eye on her,' replied the officer.

On board the cruiser from which the trawler's destiny was being controlled, the forward-looking bow camera showed only an open sea.

On the bridge of MV Orion, the lookout was becoming increasingly anxious as he peered into the darkness through powerful binoculars, watching what he could now see was a small trawler getting closer and closer.

'The small vessel to port is maintaining her course, sir,' he reported. 'And I can't see any signs of life on deck.'

'Right. Let's give her five then,' the officer said, reaching for the button that operated the ship's signalling horn. He pressed the button five times to emit the internationally recognised sound signal that officially declared 'Your intentions are unclear,' but in reality meant 'Get out of my way.'

After a few seconds the lookout reported again: 'She's still holding her course and there's still no sign of life.'

In the red-lit cabin of the trawler, the girls had heard the five blasts but could only stare at each other blankly.

'What was that?' asked one. 'It sounds close.'

It was Anna who reacted first. Even though she did not recognise the sound signal, she immediately grasped the threat it represented.

'It's a ship,' she said. 'A big ship. Very close. We all die. We all die.'

The girls all started screaming at once and the silence of the sea was split by the sound of a wail of banshees.

On the insulated, air-conditioned bridge of Orion, the sounds went unheard. 'Let's give them another five,' the Officer of the Watch said. 'And helmsman, twenty degrees to starboard.'

At the very instant the first blast was heard, the controller on the cruiser pressed a button that expanded the view of the trawler's bow camera — and his screen suddenly filled with Orion's dark hull.

'Shit,' he yelled, simultaneously moving two controls, one of which reduced the trawler's speed and the other which caused it to make a sharp turn to starboard. For what seemed an eternity Orion and the trawler ran parallel but opposing courses. Staring at the camera's ghoulish green image, the controller could have sworn the freighter was within touching distance.

The screaming girls, each convinced that death was about to strike, held each other tightly. Then the trawler started to pitch wildly as it cleared Orion's stern and crashed headlong into its wake.

The lookout on the bridge reported to the Officer of the Watch: 'She's clear astern sir. She's bouncing around a bit but she doesn't appear to be damaged.'

'Thank God for that,' replied the officer. 'Helmsman, port twenty. Let's get back to our voyage.'

He picked up the VHF radio and called the Dutch Coast Guard Communications and Co-Ordination Centre at Den Hilder, north of Amsterdam, to report his near-collision with a small fishing vessel, which was on a course of approximately 290° but with no signs of life on board. The Dutch thanked him for the information, which they then relayed to their English counterparts in Dover and Bridlington. But none of the coast guard stations had tracked the vessel on radar; there had been no other reports from other ships and nothing matching the trawler's description had filed a passage plan.

It had simply disappeared into the darkness.

In the cruiser, the controller vowed to get radar fitted and moved the controls to put the trawler back on course for England.

Gradually, the terrified girls in the trawler realised that the danger had passed; that their boat was still afloat; that they were still alive. They would never know how closely death had swept them by. As the wake of Orion receded, the motion of the trawler became less pronounced and as it did so the level of crying and moaning from its passengers dropped to the occasional blubber.

The next two hours passed uneventfully, the trawler still under the control of the cruiser five miles behind. If they had been able to see outside, the girls could have seen clusters of lights on the horizon; the lights of villages and communities scattered along the Essex coast. Their destination was in sight.

The GPS in the cruiser was showing the controller that the trawler had seven miles to run to complete its voyage. He selected a VHS radio channel that was dedicated to informal public transmissions but in practice was rarely used and even more rarely monitored by the authorities. Nevertheless, he ignored the required radio protocol, pressed the "Transmit" button and said: 'ETA 40 minutes. Rendezvous point one.'

A few seconds later the reply came: 'Rendezvous point one. Understood.' Again, no attempt to follow protocol; less opportunity for anybody listening in to make sense of the message; less opportunity to locate the source of the signal.

After exactly 40 minutes the radio in the cruiser crackled into life: 'We have contact. Boarding now.' Five miles ahead, a 27-foot long, matt-black rigid inflatable boat with two silenced outboard engines had pulled alongside the trawler and two men clambered aboard. Then another brief radio message: 'We have control.'

The controller in the cruiser acknowledged the message, switched off the remote systems and powered his boat away into the darkness.

On board the trawler, the girls listened anxiously as they heard the men climb onto the deck. Not knowing what was happening, they clung to each other as the bolt on the hatch slid back and the cover opened. A pair of sea boots appeared, followed by a pair of legs and then a torso, all encased in black waterproof sailing kit.

'Right ladies,' said the man in English and not caring if he was understood. 'Time to go.'

The eight, clutching their meagre belongings, filed on deck where another man — also dressed in black waterproofs — was standing by what looked like a ladder that disappeared over the side. 'This way, quick. Come on,' he urged. Below, they could see the RIB with two other men on board. 'Hurry up,' one of them shouted. 'We haven't got all night.'

When all eight were seated, the plastic-wrapped parcels were taken on board then the RIB silently shot off, leaving the trawler and its crew of two behind. Less than 20 minutes later, the RIB made landfall on a lonely beach on Mersea Island in Essex. The girls, bursting with dreams of new and prosperous lives, had finally made it to England.

The two crewmen helped the shivering women onto the beach then walked them a few hundred yards to where a white van was parked. A third man appeared, opened the back doors of the van and indicated that the girls should climb in. No words were exchanged. The doors slammed shut and the van lurched off.

When it stopped, Anna and her companions were just about beginning to feel warmth again in their bodies. The doors opened and the driver ushered them into a large yard surrounded by a high wire fence. They could see two large buildings, one of them with a big yellow and black sign across the front.

Those of them that could read English could see that it said Pilling Transport.

***

Light, gentle rain was falling from a leaden sky as Ray's ferry sailed into Harwich. But by the time he was driving his HGV out of the ferry

85

and onto the quayside, the drizzle had developed into a deluge. It hammered on the cab roof and exploded across the windscreen as everywhere men in waterproofs, topped off by bright yellow reflective jackets, scurried about the business of off-loading the ship and preparing it for its next voyage.

Ray was feeling very pleased with himself. He'd managed to get the lorry to Bonn and back without any mishap; he'd managed to deliver the two official cargoes he had carried, plus the unofficial one, safely; he'd had a good night's sleep and now he was on his way back home.

But his euphoria was to be short lived. As the vehicle rolled across the massive loading area, heading for the exit, a man wearing a hi-vis jacket with the letters HMRC across the front, was waving him towards the harbour's giant Customs shed. Ray's heart sank, not because he was carrying anything he shouldn't but simply because he knew it wouldn't be a quick diversion and he really wanted to be home again. To have the chance to share a drink with Jan.

As he drove through the shed doors he could see ahead of him a mobile X-ray scanner that Customs used to search the interiors of trailers, looking for anything suspicious but especially illegal immigrants. Another Customs officer, a pinch-faced man wearing square, wire-rimmed glasses, waved him forward and indicated where he had to stop.

'Good Morning Sir,' he said courteously. 'May I see your passport please?'

Ray handed the man his passport, to which he gave no more than a cursory glance.

'And what are you carrying today?'

'I'm empty mate,' Ray replied. 'I took a load of antique furniture to Bonn and then a load of rugs and carpets to Vlissingen but I didn't have anything to bring back to the UK.'

The Customs man, whose complexion was so pale he could have spent his entire life indoors, gave him an inquisitive stare that made it obvious he wasn't believed.

'And do you have any documentation to support what you have just told me?' he asked.

'Yes, of course. Hang on,' said Ray, rummaging in the driver's door pocket for the two consignment notes. He passed them down to the

Customs officer, who studied them carefully before passing them back without a word.

Then he said: 'Right, we're going to X-ray your vehicle to check its contents, so if you are carrying anything you shouldn't be, it would be in your own interest to tell me now.'

'I've told you, I'm not carrying anything at all,' Ray said.

'OK. Switch off the engine and get out of the cab please.'

As Ray closed the cab door behind him, the Customs man waved the mobile X-ray scanner forward. It was built on a mobile crane chassis, the scanner extending to one side to form a big archway. The vehicle drove slowly along the length of Ray's lorry, the scanner passing closely over the top and sides of the trailer. Then it slowly reversed.

A few minutes passed, during which neither Ray nor the Customs officer spoke. The silence was broken by another Customs man who appeared from what looked like a second cab attached to the back of the scanner.

'Peter, you need to take a look at this,' he said.

The first Customs man disappeared into the scanner cab and when he emerged again his face was set like stone. He said to Ray: 'Mr Welbourne I have to tell you that we have discovered an anomaly with your trailer and unless you can give me a satisfactory explanation I will have to detain you and impound your vehicle, do you understand?'

Ray looked genuinely puzzled. 'Yes. Well, no; not really. What do you mean, "an anomaly"?'

'The X-ray has revealed what appears to be a false bulkhead in the forward end of the trailer. What is it for?'

'I don't know. I didn't even know it was there. This is the first trip I've done in this vehicle.' Even to himself, his voice sounded panicky and unconvincing.

'Right. Just stay there,' said the Customs man before turning away and having a VHF radio conversation that Ray could not follow, hearing only the squelch of static as the dialogue switched sides.

Almost immediately a third Customs man appeared and to whom the man Ray now knew as Peter said: 'Take Mr Welbourne to the holding area. We're just going to search his vehicle.'

'Am I under arrest?' asked Ray, anxiously.

'Not at this time,' replied Peter. 'But you won't be allowed to leave until the search of your vehicle has been completed.'

Ray was taken to a small, windowless room that was bare apart from half a dozen hard-backed chairs placed around the walls. He may not have been under arrest but as he sat down he was sure he heard the sound of a key turning in the lock.

Out in the Customs shed, a rummage team set about searching the HGV from end to end, leaving nothing to chance, probing every nook and cranny. When that was complete, they set about taking apart the false bulkhead found by the X-ray. The whole process had taken almost three hours but when the bulkhead was finally removed, the team leader radioed Peter.

'I think we've found what you were looking for,' was all he said.

When Peter joined the team in the trailer, the leader pointed to the area behind the bulkhead. 'There you are...'

On the floor were two discarded sweet wrappers. And a sugar bag-sized package, sheathed in black plastic, which had been ripped open, allowing white powder to spill out.

CHAPTER 11

For the briefest of instants, so brief that no clock could have recorded it, Ray thought of identifying himself to the two policemen sent to arrest him. 'I'm actually a Detective Chief Inspector, seconded to the National Crime Agency and working undercover,' he could have said and gone back to running the Major Inquiry Team in Bradford, West Yorkshire.

But he didn't say anything because he knew if he did it would have blown the entire operation to bring down the Hydra. And it also sounded so implausible that the two young constables might not have been too careful about the way they handled him in and out of their car.

And so he found himself in Harwich's red-brick police station standing in front of the charge office sergeant, who took his personal details then told him he was being bailed "pending further enquiries."

'What does that mean then?' Ray asked the sergeant, who had tufts of silver hair growing from each ear, above which grew a monk-like tonsure that was also silver.

'It means you are free to go while the Crown Prosecution Service decides whether there's enough evidence to charge you under the Misuse of Drugs Act 1971 with possession of Class A drugs with intent to supply,' he replied. 'If they do decide to charge you, you'll be brought to trial. If they don't, no further action will be taken. But that doesn't mean we can't re-arrest you if we find more evidence in the future.

'Oh and by the way, the maximum sentence for possession of Class A with intent is life.'

'Great. Thanks a lot pal,' said Ray flippantly. 'When do we get our lorry back?'

'You'll need to speak to Customs about that but I suspect they'll want to keep the trailer pending the CPS's decision,' said the Sergeant.

'Where's my passport?' he asked.

'Customs are keeping that too,' he was told. 'It's a condition of bail.'

Outside on the pavement, Ray stood for a moment, gathering his thoughts and breathing deeply, trying to think of any reason why Customs should have picked on him and his truck. As he pondered his mobile phone rang.

'Welbourne, what the fuck's going on? Customs have just told me they've impounded our truck.'

'Good morning Mike. Yes, I'm very well thank you,' was Ray's sarcastic response to his irate boss. 'Actually I was hoping you might be able to tell me what the fuck's going on.'

'Where are you now?' barked Pilling, ignoring Ray's caustic comment.

'Outside Harwich nick.'

'Wait there. I'll get someone to pick you up.' The line went dead.

Ray looked around in vain for a pub but there was none in sight and he wasn't in the mood to go searching for one. Diagonally opposite the police station he could see a park. The rain had stopped and it was reasonably warm so the park won. Five minutes later he was nodding gently on a park bench.

It seemed to him that he had been asleep only seconds when the jangling of his mobile roused him with a start. George Curtis was on the other end. 'I'm outside Harwich nick, where the fuck are you?' he growled.

'In the park opposite. Stay there, I'll find you,' said Ray, dragging himself to his feet.

From the entrance to the park, he could see a white Mercedes S Class saloon and decided it was Curtis, although he had no idea to whom the car belonged. As he approached, the boot lid lifted, apparently of its own accord, so he threw in his overnight bag and climbed wearily into the passenger set.

'What the fucking hell went wrong?' were Curtis's opening words. 'Mike's blazing.'

Ray stared at him for a fraction of a second, deciding whether to start the argument here or wait until he saw Mike Pilling. He decided to wait.

'Nothing "went wrong" as you put it,' he replied calmly. 'I did everything I was supposed to do. I stuck to the timetable and didn't speak to anyone I shouldn't have. But Customs picked on me for some reason.'

'So why did they impound the lorry and have you arrested?'

'They said they had found a false bulkhead in the trailer and a quantity of drugs,' Ray said.

Curtis made no response other than a low chuckle.

'Look, it's not funny,' Ray snarled. 'I was arrested on suspicion of possession of Class A drugs with intent to supply. I could be looking at life here.'

'Don't worry,' replied Curtis. 'It won't come to that.'

***

Around half an hour later, the Mercedes pulled into Pilling Transport's depot. In the office Summer gave Ray a look that could almost have been one of compassion.

'Christ Ray, you look like a badger's arse,' she said. 'Do you want a cup of tea?'

Before he got chance to answer, Mike Pilling answered for him. 'He hasn't got time for tea. He's got some explaining to do,' he bawled from his office.' Get in here now Welbourne.'

Ray murmured: 'Maybe later eh?' as he passed Summer's desk.

It was immediately obvious that Pilling was indeed "blazing." His pock-marked complexion was puce and the dark bags under his eyes were streaked with yellow. His hands shook, although Ray could not be certain whether it was with anger or an after-effect of over indulgence in recreational drugs, booze or possibly both. His voice, though, remained inexplicably calm.

'Right Welbourne, sit down and tell me what the fuck happened.'

For the next 20 minutes, Ray described every detail of his trip; his meeting with the Hell's Angel lookalikes in Bonn; how Anna was thrown into his cab, giving away the secret of his true cargo; his journey to Vlissingen; the unloading of the trailer there and his subsequent passage back to Harwich.

'When I got back to Harwich, Customs pulled me over and put a rummage team through the lorry, even though I told them I was empty,' Ray said. 'Then they X-rayed the trailer and found the false partition and a parcel of something they thought was Class A drugs. They called for PC Plod and I was nicked. It just felt like I'd been set-up.'

'Believe me, you weren't,' Pilling replied. 'You weren't supposed to know anything about what you were carrying other than what was on the consignment notes. Are you sure you didn't tell anybody about having the girl in the cab?'

'Mike, I didn't even speak to anybody other than the check-in girl at the Hook,' said Ray. 'I went straight to my cabin because I was so tired.

The next person I spoke to was the Customs man when we landed at Harwich.'

'Well something's gone badly wrong and when I find out whose fault it is they're dead,' Pilling said, clenching his fists. 'I just hope it's not that bastard Chiswell after all I've done for him. But we're all deeply in the shit here and I'm going to have to call in a favour. A big one. And if I can't, well, none of us will be farting in church for a while.'

'What are you going to do?'

'You're better off not knowing,' Pilling replied. 'In fact, the less you know, the happier I am. Now, get out of my sight — and tell Summer to make me some coffee.'

Back in the main office, he got no further than 'Mike says...' before Summer cut him dead. 'I know. I heard him,' she said, rising from her desk and heading for the small kitchen area. 'D'you want one too?'

'I'll have tea if it's no trouble,' said Ray.

'I wouldn't have asked if it was any trouble,' she snapped back.

He still couldn't understand this young woman, upon whom Mike Pilling seemed to place so much reliance. Underneath the caked make-up and the dyed hair, he thought she was probably quite attractive. She demonstrated no discernible dress sense, but then again she worked in an environment that managed to be both dusty and oily at the same time. Yet she was aggressive to the point where if she had been a dog, she would probably have had to wear a muzzle. She treated every question, every statement, every request as if it was a challenge to combat.

It would be a while yet before Ray realised that Summer was suffering from a paranoia induced by over-indulgence in marijuana.

He had nothing to do so he took his mug of tea to an empty desk and pretended to be doing some paper work. He rapidly got bored with that so he found a couple of back copies of "Commercial Motor" magazine and started reading. He read but didn't absorb. Instead he had one eye on the clock, which was ticking down towards five o'clock about as quickly as treacle in a fridge. When it finally reached the departing hour, he threw on his jacket, swept up his overnight bag and headed for the door.

'See you on Monday Summer,' he called. 'Have a great weekend.'

'And you,' she said to his retreating back, without imparting one iota of sincerity or meaningfulness.

From the privacy of his car, he rang Jan. She answered virtually instantly, as if she had been expecting his call. 'I need to see you as soon as,' he said. 'Can we meet tomorrow?'

'Course we can,' she replied, the first cheery voice he had heard in many days. 'Why don't we go back to that Thai restaurant we went to? My treat.'

'Sounds fine to me but I might pull rank on you over the bill,' Ray answered. 'Shall we meet in that pub where they had live music? About eight?'

'See you there,' was all she said. And the line went dead.

Ray went back to his new flat, found a ready meal in the freezer and cracked open a bottle of Duval, his favourite Belgian beer, while it warmed up. He watched television with unseeing eyes while he ate from a tray balanced on his knees. Then he treated himself to a second bottle of Duval and before he knew it, he was slumbering soundly. When the insistent buzzing of his mobile roused him, he had no idea how long he had been sleeping.

'Welbourne, it's Mike Pilling,' the unmistakable voice said. 'Customs have released our tractor unit, but they're hanging on to the trailer for a while. We can pick it up tomorrow. Or rather, you can pick it up tomorrow. Meet me at the depot at nine and I'll give you a set of keys so you can put the bloody thing away when you get back.'

No ifs, buts or maybes. Just a straight-forward order.

It was still not long after eight but Ray decided that his bed was the only place he wanted to be. Later he remembered falling asleep almost at the moment his head hit the pillow. And he slept the clock around.

Next morning, he made it to the depot literally a few seconds behind Pilling.

'Keep these with you 'till Monday,' Pilling said, thrusting the depot keys into Ray's hand. 'And don't fucking lose 'em.'

It wouldn't matter if I did, thought Ray. *I've got a set of my own.*

'And when you get back don't bother coming to the office. It's off limits today. To everyone.'

Ray had learned better than to ask why.

***

To a casual observer, Ray and Jan looked like the perfect loving couple. In the pub she greeted him with a kiss on the cheek that lingered just a bit too long to be a hello peck between friends. When they left, Jan took his arm and was still clinging to it when they arrived in the restaurant, where they were shown to a discreet table that shielded them from the view of passers-by. Throughout the meal she spent long minutes simply staring into his eyes and the pair of them seemed to be very comfortable and content in each other's company.

What no one else knew was that beneath the dewy stares and inviting smiles, important information was being exchanged. Ray gave Jan a full briefing on his journey to Bonn and how his truck had been used to smuggle eight girls to Vlissingen, from where he knew their destination was England but not how they would get there. He told her about Anna and how desperately sad he felt for her; how he wanted to warn about what she was heading into. He told her about being pulled by Customs and then being arrested on suspicion of possession of Class A drugs with intent to supply; how the truck had been impounded and how he had been back to Harwich early that day to collect the tractor unit.

He also told her that he planned to return to the depot the next day and using the keys Pilling had given him, inspect the shed that until now had been a closed book; the shed where Curtis had told him Pilling kept his collection of historic cars but where Ray suspected he would find more secrets of the Hydra operation.

From the restaurant, they returned, arm-in-arm, to the pub where, by now, a four-piece band was belting out country music at ear-splitting levels that made conversation impossible. They took their drinks as far into a corner as they could get but the music was still intrusively loud.

'We could always go somewhere more quiet,' Jan yelled into Ray's ear.

'Like where?'

'Like my place.'

This time there was no argument and after a brisk 15 minute walk, Ray followed her through the door of a spacious, well-appointed first-floor flat. He flopped down on a wide, three-seat sofa and took in the flat screen television complete with a satellite receiver, sheepskin rug and solid oak dining suite. Through an open door he could see a king-sized bed with appealingly plump pillows and fluffy duvet.

'What do you fancy to drink,' Jan shouted from the kitchen. 'I've got just about everything you can think of.'

'I'll stick with beer,' answered Ray. 'I need to have my wits about me tomorrow.'

She appeared with two bottles of designer-label Italian beer and sat down next to him.

By way of conversation he said: 'This is a nice place. How did you manage to find it?'

'I didn't,' said Jan. 'The NCA found it and furnished it. They also pay the rent through a new bank account they set up for me. It is very nice but it can get boring. All I have to do is hang about and wait for you to make contact, which — as I'm sure you're aware — isn't that often. So when you do I need to make the most of it.'

She put down the beer bottle, took his face in her hands and kissed him squarely and fully on the mouth, pushing her tongue between his lips and moving her body across his as she did so.

Ray did not resist but neither did he respond.

After a few seconds she pulled away and looked him in the eyes.

'Jan, look, I'm really sorry,' he began, 'but you know this will never work. I like you a lot and I admire your professionalism and that's why it can't go any further. We're here to do a job and even though we're supposed to be lovers, I'm still technically your senior officer. Just think what The Sun would make of this if they found out — "Taxpayers' Funded Cop's Love Nest" would be the least of it.'

Her big, brown eyes brimmed with tears. As they began to roll down her cheeks, she rushed for the bedroom and slammed the door behind her.

When she hadn't reappeared in ten minutes, Ray picked up his jacket and slipped out into the night.

Outside he had no idea where he was so he began walking back towards the pub. When he got there he realised he should probably have taken more notice of the route the taxi that had taken him there followed. From the pub he just carried on walking until he came to a private hire car parked at the side of the road, the driver taking a nap.

He tapped on the window and asked the startled driver if he could take him to the hospital gates, from where he knew his flat was only a stone's throw. He was very wary of giving his address to anybody who did not absolutely need to have it.

'Well, I could,' the driver replied. 'Except you wouldn't be insured because you haven't booked me through the office. Plus, it's about 200 yards up on the right. You could walk there before you get your seat belt fastened.'

***

The following morning he awoke feeling guilty about the way he had brushed aside Jan's advances. He knew he had done the right thing but, with hindsight, he thought he could have handled it more diplomatically. He would apologise. But first he had a job to do.

The Pilling Transport depot was, as he had hoped, deserted on this quiet Sunday morning. Using the keys that Mike Pilling had given him, he opened the gates and drove inside. Just in case anyone was around, his cover story was that he had lost his wallet and was checking he hadn't dropped in the cab of his truck. Not very original but vaguely plausible.

He unlocked the office and made his way to the far corner where there was another door, permanently locked, that Summer had told him led into "Mike's Shed." He was gambling on the key being part of the collection that Pilling had given him. Sure enough, the fourth one he tried turned the tumblers and the tenon slid back.

Inside, he found the centre of the shed occupied by three cars, each under tightly fitted dust covers, which he decided against disturbing. Along one wall was a row of what looked like four small offices, each — apart from the very end one — with a window looking out into the shed. None of them looked like they were used. A flight of wide wooden steps led to a balcony that ran the length of the offices.

Gingerly he climbed the steps and found himself facing a door which yielded at the turn of the handle. It was pitch black inside. He fumbled for a light switch and the place filled with the harsh, bright light of overhead neon-strip lighting. It took Ray several seconds to take in what he was seeing.

To his left was a kitchen sink, a small food preparation area and an oven. The middle of the room was taken up by three rows of bunks and at the far end, what appeared to be a small bathroom. Discarded pizza boxes spilled from a waste-bin and dirty cups were piled in the sink. It was obvious that someone, probably several people, had been living there recently. And it didn't take a detective's brain to work out who.

Ray wondered how many more hideaways like this the Hydra had in which it concealed its smuggled young women.

He used his phone camera to photograph the evidence then he went back downstairs, straight to the end, windowless, office. It was locked but by trial and error with the bunch of keys, he managed to get inside. This time the light switch triggered a much more subtle shade of light, revealing a professionally equipped photographic studio. Against the end wall a roll of white back-drop paper hung down from the ceiling and spread about three metres across the floor. Two powerful Elinchrom studio flashes, one fitted with a softbox diffuser and the other with a reflector umbrella, stood angled in towards the back-drop. In the centre was a tripod carrying what Ray recognised as a top-of-range Nikon D4 digital SLR camera.

Curiosity got the better of him. He switched the camera on and pressed the button that would reveal the images stored on its memory card. One after another the images appeared. All of them were of girls in their early 20s. All of them in various states of undress. All of them forcing a smile.

For reasons he would never be able to explain, Ray carried on flicking back through the increasingly explicit pictures until one stopped him dead.

This girl was naked apart from a pair of black stockings. The composition of the image left nothing to the imagination but he was struck by how frail she appeared; how thin and under-nourished she was. Beneath her tiny breasts, her ribs were clearly visible.

But it was her face that had the most impact on him. This girl, too, was forcing a smile. Her skin was pale and taut. Her eyes were dead, yet even in their deadness they managed to convey fear.

The face hypnotised him because it was a face he knew.

He was staring at the face of Anna.

CHAPTER 12

Ray knew there would be more images of Anna but he couldn't bring himself to look at them. Instead he used his phone camera to copy the picture from the small screen. Then he scrolled forward and copied one image of each of the other seven girls. Each image was stamped with the date and time it had been taken, showing they had all been taken the previous day. No wonder Pilling had told him the office block was off-limits.

He knew that what he had was only a small fragment of evidence; evidence that would be bolstered by the fact that he could testify that a young girl who had told him she was being smuggled into a new life in England was instead being groomed for a future as a sex worker.

Back at his flat he copied all the photographs from his phone to his laptop and then to the flash drive that was still hidden inside a sock before deleting them from both devices.

He cracked the crown cork off a bottle of Duval and sat staring at his phone, as if willing it to ring. He knew that he had to talk to Jan; that he had to hand over the flash drive and tell her about everything he had found inside Pilling Transport's depot. But he knew the kind of reception he'd get — arctic would just about cover it. How much easier things would be if she rang him. But deep down he also knew that was never going to happen. His only choice was to bite the bullet, apologise profusely and swear to himself that he would never again be coerced into a potentially compromising situation with Jan.

She answered on the fourth ring with a terse: 'Yes boss.'

'Hi Jan, it's me,' he said, unnecessarily. 'Listen, I need to apologise to you for the misunderstanding last night, it's just...'

'There was no misunderstanding,' she snapped. 'I wanted to shag you. You didn't want to shag me. That's all. End of. Now, shall we be grown up about it and move on?'

Ray had never heard her be so blunt and forthright. Her frankness took him by surprise.

'Er, yes... yes, of course,' he replied. 'We need to meet. I have something you need to pass on. You choose.'

'There's a pub called the Goat and Boot on East Hill. I'll see you there in an hour.' And she hung up.

The taxi dropped him at the pub a good 15 minutes before they were due to meet. Inside, he was delighted to find it served his favourite Greene King IPA so he took a pint into the beamed-ceilinged lounge and sat alongside the huge brick-built fireplace, as far from the door as he could.

Jan was on time to the second, almost as if she had been standing outside waiting for the clock to tick down to the meeting hour. She sat down next to him and gave him a perfunctory peck on the cheek.

'That's just for appearances,' she whispered and then, more loudly: 'I'll have a pint of what you're drinking, thank you.'

When Ray returned with her drink he sat down next to her and felt her slide away, imperceptibly but enough to make a point.

'Jan, before we go any further I want to apologise again...'

'I don't want to talk about it,' she interrupted. 'It was a stupid thing to do and it won't happen again. From now on we're just colleagues. Agreed?'

'Agreed,' he nodded.

'Now, what have you got for me?'

He took the flash drive from his pocket and passed it to her by taking hold of her hand, which she quickly pulled away. 'On there are pictures of everything I've found at Pilling's depot,' he said. 'As well as the cannabis farm, there are shots of a dormitory style set-up in one of the main buildings. There are also some pretty explicit pictures of eight girls. One of them is Anna, the girl I told you about that rode in the cab with me from Bonn. I assume the other seven are the girls who were hidden in the trailer. The quality's not brilliant because they're copied from an SLR review screen but at least they link Pillings with smuggled people, girls especially.'

'Do you have anything else?' Jan asked.

'Not that's materially useful,' said Ray. 'I'm sweating on whether the CPS will charge me with possession with intent to supply. Pilling said it wouldn't happen because he'd call in a few favours. That's obviously to protect his back, not mine. But if he does what he says, it will be interesting to see if the chain of decision making can be traced. It might help identify who the Hydra has got its claws into.'

'OK. I'll let the right people know what you've got,' said Jan, draining her pint. 'So if that's it, I'll love you and leave you, as my old gran used to say. Ring me yeah?'

Before Ray got the chance to reply, she was gone and he was left alone with a half-drunk pint.

***

The head of the Crown Prosecution Service's Eastern Region was a busy woman. The region's population numbered almost four million, protected by four county police forces, for each of which the CPS was responsible for advising and reviewing potential prosecutions, determining what charges should be brought, preparing cases and presenting the evidence in court. All with a staff of less than 300.

The crimes they dealt with ranged from the everyday burglaries and thefts to assaults, rapes and murders. And so when Cheryl Bonicki received a telephone call from the Principal Legal Advisor at CPS headquarters in London, she was dumbfounded.

'Mizz Bonicki,' Robert Boulton began, 'I believe you are dealing with a case of possession of Class A with intent. Chap name of Welbourne. From Colchester.'

'I'm not personally familiar with the case Mr Boulton but how can I help?'

'We don't think it's in the public interest to proceed. We want you not to bring any charges.'

'I'm not in a position to argue because I haven't seen the papers,' she said. 'But when you say "we" who are you referring to exactly?'

'Actually, the decision is mine and mine alone, in my capacity as Principal Legal Advisor and, therefore, your superior.'

'I don't understand why you personally should take an interest in what is a relatively trivial case.'

'I've just told you. We don't think it is in the public interest.'

'But why on earth not? Surely we're sending out dangerous messages.'

'Mizz Bonicki, this is not a topic for discussion,' said Boulton. 'What I have just given you is an instruction not a suggestion.'

For a second she struggled to suppress the frustration welling up inside her. 'Then may I, once again, ask why you are so interested in this case?'

'No, you may not,' he replied. 'Goodbye Mizz Bonicki.'

***

As he put down the phone, Robert Boulton wiped the sweat from his brow with an immaculately pressed, snow-white handkerchief. It was done and now he could breathe easily again. That is, if the bitch did as she'd been told. If she didn't, he was so deeply in the shit there was no way out. What would follow would be public humiliation, shame, the break-up of his marriage, the end of his comfortable family life and the end of his career.

What Cheryl Bonicki had no way of knowing when she picked up the phone to find Robert Boulton on the other end, was the pressure that had been put on him. She was right when she described the charge that Ray Welbourne faced as a relatively minor one. But to the Hydra it had the potential for disaster. They could not afford for the spotlight of publicity that would be generated by a court case to fall on Pilling Transport, so it not only had to be extinguished, it had to be prevented from being switched on at all.

Boulton had been sitting at his desk in his spacious office in Southwark Bridge when his direct line rang. The voice was dark and menacing with a barely discernible accent that nonetheless gave it the precision that goes with speaking a language that has been learned rather than inherited.

'Mr Boulton, I represent the people to whom you owe a great debt,' the man had said. 'The people who have arranged for you several illicit rendezvous with girls of — how can I put this? — a certain compliant nature. Do you understand me?'

'I'm... I'm not sure; I'm not sure I do,' Boulton had stumbled.

'Oh, I think you do Mr Boulton,' the voice replied. 'Why, only last week we organised a party for four people in a very expensive London hotel room. You had asked for a blonde, a brunette and a redhead. It took a while to find the right girls but we did. I am sure the more lurid newspapers would find the video of that party very interesting indeed, not to mention your wife and colleagues. And then there was that week you spent in Manchester when we...'

'Yes, yes. Alright. I know who you are. What do you want?'

'Perhaps a little civility and a touch of humility might help to begin with Mr Boulton. We need you to stop a prosecution going ahead.'

'I can't; not after the last time. I came close to losing my job over that maniac killer you employed.'

There was an audible sigh down the phone before the voice continued: 'Well, Mr Boulton, let me put it this way. If you do not help us, you certainly will lose your job this time, along with everything else you hold dear. We already have a DVD compilation of all your extra-marital activities and copies prepared for every national newspaper and TV station, Downing Street, the Director of Public Prosecutions, the Commissioner of the Metropolitan Police, your boss and an extra-special one with added stills for your wife. They can be in the post within ten minutes of me ending this call. Now, how do you want to proceed?'

'I can see I don't have a choice in the matter,' replied Boulton. 'What is it you want me to do?'

Less than an hour later Robert Boulton had identified the case being prepared against Ray and was picking up the phone to Cheryl Bonicki.

***

Ray was out in the Transit doing yet another drug delivery run, this time to the East Midlands, when he answered his mobile to Mike Pilling.

'I told you there was nothing to worry about,' Pilling said. 'I've just been told the CPS has recommended no action against you on the grounds that a prosecution would not be in the public interest. That means there will be no charges against the company either.'

'Thanks Mike, that's great news. It's a great weight off my mind,' Ray said. 'Does that mean I can have my passport back too?'

'Yes it does. We're picking up the trailer tomorrow so I'll get it collected at the same time. I don't want you going anywhere near HMRC at Harwich for a while. I know they're spitting blood. They thought they had us with the trailer and the drug spill but, mysteriously, somebody at the top disagrees. See you later.'

The relief sank slowly through Ray's veins, taking with it the adrenalin that had kept him awake the past few days. He pulled into the next lay-by, locked the van's doors from inside and fell asleep.

When he awoke, he knew he had to contact Jan. The information he now had was the first positive step in breaking the grasp of the Hydra. Armed with what he would relay to the NCA, agents could now trace the process which led to charges against him and Pilling transport being dropped; a process that he suspected would lead to the very top.

Jan again chose the Goat and Boot for their meeting. This time it was well into the evening and the pub was very busy. Neither Jan nor Ray had known it was quiz night and they struggled to find a quiet corner where their conversation could not be ear-wigged.

'Why do we have to keep doing this?' Jan asked as he sat down next to her with their drinks.

'Doing what?'

'Meeting. Why can't you just tell me what you need to on the phone?'

'Because telephone conversations can be intercepted; voicemails can be hacked remember.'

'Yes, but we're both using mobiles provided to us by the people we work for. That should be just about as secure as you can get.'

Ray half turned towards her and lowered his voice. 'I know that Jan, but do you really trust them?' he asked. 'If the Hydra's reach is as long as the intelligence indicates, isn't it just feasible that the NCA has been compromised too?'

'Christ Ray, that's bordering on paranoia.'

'Maybe it is,' said Ray. 'But I'd rather not take the risk. It's my neck out there if somebody in the organisation turns out bad. Now, just for my own peace of mind, who have you been reporting to?'

'Wilpshire and Copeland.'

'Good. Keep it that way. Don't talk to anybody else. And as a precaution, keep a written record of everything you hand over and everything you say and who you give it or say it to,' he said. 'If things go tits-up I don't want the shit pouring over both our heads.'

'D'you know, that's almost the most romantic thing anybody's every said to me,' said Jan with a grin.

He almost believed he had been forgiven.

***

At the National Crime Agency's London headquarters, Bernard Copeland, Director of Border Policing Command, was bubbling with excitement at the information he had just received from Jan Holroyd. The few people who saw him would later say he was practically dancing down the corridor towards the office occupied by Michael Wilpshire, the Director of the Organised Crime Command. In his hand he carried a CD containing copies of all the images Ray had taken inside Pilling Transport, as well as those taken by HMRC at Harwich; a copy of Ray's charge sheet from Essex Police plus a copy of the decision by CPS

Eastern Region that the public interest would not be served by proceeding with the charges.

'This is it Mike,' he enthused, waving the documents in the air as he burst into Wilpshire's office. 'This is it.'

Wilpshire looked up, startled, from the report he was reading. 'This is what Bernard? What is it that's got you so excited?' he asked.

'The first real piece of evidence against the Hydra. Wilson's come up with the goods. We'll need a lot more but at least we've got something to get started on,' answered Copeland.

He flopped into a leather chair on the opposite side of Wilpshire's desk and tossed the pile of documents onto to its polished oak surface. 'It's all there,' he began. 'Wilson was sent to Germany with a trailer that apparently had a secret compartment. According to his report he knew nothing about its existence until a young Albanian girl was put into his cab for another delivery he was due to make in Vlissingen. It was her that spilt the beans. Told him she was being smuggled to England to start a new life and that she had seven mates hidden in his trailer.

'When he got to Harwich, he knew he was empty but he got pulled by Customs. They found the compartment with a bursted package of cocaine in it. They had him arrested and he was charged with possession of Class A drugs with intent to supply. Then the head of CPS Eastern region suddenly decides there's no public interest in pursuing the charges. So they're dropped, Wilson's a free man and Pilling Transport get their vehicle back.'

Wilpshire took a few seconds to absorb what he had been told. 'So, are you saying that someone leaned on the CPS?'

'That's exactly what I'm saying,' replied Copeland. 'And it gets better. On that CD are some pretty nasty pictures of young girls; eight of them in total. Wilson has identified one of them as the Albanian girl who travelled with him from Bonn to Vlissingen. All the pictures are date and time stamped and show they were taken last Saturday — the day before Wilson discovered a dormitory and a professionally equipped photographic studio in Pilling Transport's depot.

'What we don't know, as yet, is how the girls who we believe were hidden in Wilson's trailer got into the UK. Nor do we know what prompted HMRC to stop and search it when it arrived in Harwich. But we're working on it.'

A smile slowly spread Mike Wilpshire's mouth, revealing immaculate white teeth. 'Excellent stuff Bernard,' he said. 'We need to get somebody up to Chelmsford to interview the head of CPS Eastern and take a statement. He or she needs to be left in no doubt that they have to tell us why the decision to drop charges against Wilson was taken and if any pressure was put upon them, they have to tell us by whom.

'And I'm sure I don't have to remind you that whoever goes must not know that Wilson is under-cover. His life hangs on his anonymity.'

CHAPTER 13

Cheryl Bonicki was left feeling bullied — and sullied — by her telephone encounter with Robert Boulton. She knew that the Principal Legal Advisor must have had an ulterior motive in ordering her to drop the charges against Ray Welbourne and, therefore, against his employer, Pilling Transport. She knew the decision was wrong, legally and morally. It went against everything she had ever been taught; against every iota of her own moral code; against everything she knew to be right. And she also knew there was nothing she could do about it.

All through her life, her parents and grandparents had instilled in her the principles of truth, justice and fair play. Her grandparents had fled from Poland to England in 1938 to escape the Nazi pogroms against Jews and had found sanctuary in the East End of London, where they survived the Blitz. Her parents had scraped together enough money to put a deposit on a small terraced house in Streatham, South London, where Cheryl, an only child, was born and raised. She had excelled at school, with more than one of her teachers remarking what an astute participant she was in class debates, so it came as no surprise when she gained a university place and opted to study law.

After qualifying as a solicitor, she joined a small law firm in Croydon where she rapidly established a reputation as a tenacious defence lawyer in the town's magistrates' courts. Eventually she came to the attention of the Crown Prosecution Service who offered her a giant pay rise to switch sides and prosecute criminals instead of defending them. The great god money won out and now, in her early 40s, she lived a very comfortable life as head of the CPS's Eastern Region, with a family of her own and a smart detached home on the outskirts of Chelmsford.

But she still clung to the principles planted in her all those years ago by her parents and grandparents.

And so it was that on the morning her secretary rang to say that there were two gentlemen downstairs from the National Crime Agency who wanted to speak to her on a matter they wouldn't reveal but they didn't have an appointment, she answered simply: 'Better send them up then.'

Having never previously dealt with the NCA, she had no idea what to expect, but when the two men were shown into her office, she could have been looking at two peas in a pod. Both were in their mid-30s; both were of average height and build; both were wearing grey suits with white shirts and dark ties. They were anonymous.

One of them extended his hand and said: 'Mrs Bonicki, good of you to see us. My name is Patrick Bird and this is my colleague Josh Sandford. We're from the National Crime Agency and we believe you can help us with some inquiries we're making.'

'Good morning gentlemen. I'll do whatever I can to help but, first, can I interest you in tea or coffee?' she asked.

'No thank you. We'd prefer to get on,' replied Bird. 'We understand you recently took the decision not to proceed with a case involving a man named Ray Welbourne, who had been charged with possession of Class A drugs with intent to supply. Can you tell us why that decision was taken?'

Cheryl hesitated while her lawyer's brain swiftly analysed what she had just been told.

'Am I under investigation?'

Sandford answered: 'Not at all Mrs Boniciki. We are here to simply establish the background to the decision to try to help us understand why it was taken.'

She picked up a plastic automatic pencil from her desk, rolling it between her fingers as she sat back in her chair, eyeing the two agents carefully. 'Well, quite simply, if you're asking why the decision not to proceed was taken, you're asking the wrong person.'

'What do you mean?' asked Sandford. 'You are head of Eastern Region aren't you?'

'Yes I am,' she said. 'But the decision was taken much farther up the food chain than me. I was just told to implement it.'

The two men glanced at each other, a look of puzzlement on their faces. 'I'm sorry Mrs Bonicki, we're not following you,' said Bird.

'I got a telephone call from a man called Robert Boulton, who is the Principal Legal Advisor at CPS headquarters in London,' she said. 'He told me that he didn't think the public interest would be served by proceeding with the case. I asked him why but he wouldn't answer. I asked him why he was taking an interest in such a relatively minor case and he wouldn't answer that either. In fact, he wouldn't answer any question I asked him.'

'But he asked you, in effect, to drop the charges,' Bird said.

'The phrase he used — and I remember this very clearly — was "What I have just given you is an instruction not a suggestion." He wouldn't listen to any argument I tried to advance and flatly refused to discuss his reasons. He is my superior so I didn't have any choice but to comply.'

Sandford asked: 'Had you had any previous dealings with Mr Boulton?'

'None whatsoever,' Cheryl answered. 'I knew who he was, of course, but I had never spoken to him before.'

'So why do you think he was interested in what, as you say, was a relatively minor offence?' asked Sandford.

'I have absolutely no idea. He wouldn't discuss it with me.'

Bird added: 'Do you have any links with Ray Welbourne?'

'None at all. I wasn't even aware of the case until Boulton called me.'

'Have you ever heard of, or had any dealings with, a company called Pilling Transport or its boss, Mike Pilling?'

'No. Neither,' she answered.

Bird made a movement that could have been interpreted as a shrug of the shoulders.

'Well, thank you for your time, Mrs Bonicki, you've been very helpful,' he said. 'If there's anything else we need, we'll be back in touch. But, in the meantime, please don't discuss this interview with anybody. It's part of an on-going investigation and I wouldn't like you to unwittingly compromise it.'

As the two men closed her office door behind them, Cheryl was left open-mouthed. First of all she was bullied and now she was being threatened. All over a straight-forward charge of possession with intent. The one thing she was sure of was that nobody was telling her the whole truth.

Bird and Sandford kept quiet until they were inside the privacy of their car.

'What do you think?' asked Bird.

'I think she's telling us the truth,' Sandford replied. 'It looks certain that she was leaned on by this Boulton geezer. All we need to find out is why.'

Bird pondered for a moment. 'Yeah, I think you're right. I reckon we should pay Mr Boulton a surprise visit tomorrow. But you know what? Something she said has got me thinking. Why *has* a charge being dropped against a small-face drug dealer taken on such importance? Nobody has explained that have they?'

'No they haven't. It's a good point but I'm not going to hold my breath waiting for an answer.'

***

Robert Boulton felt a shiver run down his spine, quickly followed by the sensation that his skin was tingling all over his body as the adrenalin, released by the shock of what he had just been told, coursed through his veins. His secretary may well have told him what it was the two visitors wanted but, if she had, it had been blanked from his mind; blanked by three words: National Crime Agency.

How did they know? How much did they know? That bitch in Chelmsford must have blabbed. What did she tell them? National Crime Agency. Serious shit. Stonewall them. The only chance.

By the time Bird and Sandford were ushered into his office, Boulton was a picture of calmness, at least on the outside. Inside, every nerve-ending jangled; he was alert to every minor movement, every gesture. He felt like he had X-ray vision.

'Gentlemen, how can I help you?' he asked, gesturing expansively towards the two, expensive leather chairs that fronted his wide, kidney-shaped solid oak desk. There were no introductions, no invitations to tea or coffee; none of the niceties the two agents had received from Cheryl Bonicki.

Bird responded in kind. 'We're investigating the circumstances that led to a charge of possession of Class A drugs with intent to supply being dropped against a man called Ray Welbourne from Colchester. We understand you were instrumental in having the charges dropped. Can you tell us why?'

So, it was that bitch.

'The simple fact is that we, the Crown Prosecution Service, didn't feel the public interest would be served by pursuing a fairly low-key charge against an individual and his employer, a business which conducts a lot of trade throughout Europe, to the benefit of UK plc.'

'Was it your decision alone or did someone instruct you in the matter,' asked Sandford, lapsing into his best solicitor-speak.

For a few seconds, Boulton looked blankly at the two men. 'I'm sorry but I don't see the relevance of that question,' he said. 'I've just told you, it was decided prosecution was not in the public interest.'

'It's a question that's highly relevant to our inquiry,' said Sandford. 'We need to establish who took the decision. Was it you acting alone or in concert with one or more other people?'

Boulton felt his heart racing. 'I'm afraid that's not a question I can answer,' he said.

'Can't or won't?' snapped Sandford. 'What are you trying to hide Mr Boulton?'

'I don't like your tone,' he bluntly replied.

Sensing the interview was slipping away, Bird came back with: 'Let me put it another way Mr Boulton. Is the reason you will not answer our questions that you are trying to protect someone.'

'Look, I've already said I am not at liberty to answer.'

'But what we're having difficulty understanding is why you, as Principal Legal Advisor to the Crown Prosecution service would have the slightest interest in a what is, let's face it, a run-of-the-mill case. Unless, of course, someone ordered you to take an interest.'

The blush spread rapidly and completely over Boulton's face, even taking in his not insubstantial ears.

'Right that's it,' he fumed. 'I'm not going to take any more of your innuendoes. This interview is terminated. Good day gentlemen.'

Bird smiled a wry smile. 'Very well Mr Boulton, if that's what you wish. But it may well be that we want to speak to you again so, if we do, next time you will be arrested and taken to the nearest convenient police station. And you also don't need me to tell you that we would be absolutely powerless to stop the newspapers taking photographs outside the building.'

'Are you threatening me?'

'Not at all sir. I'm merely pointing out to you the potential for adverse Press coverage, should it be necessary to arrest you.'

'And the charge would be?'

'I hadn't really thought about it. But I think conspiracy to pervert the course of justice might be a good starting point.' He flicked a business card from his top pocket onto Boulton's desk. 'If you should change your mind, you will get either of us on that number. Goodbye Mr Boulton.'

As the office door closed behind them, Boulton slumped into his chair, his heart racing, images too terrible to contemplate churning around his brain, the consequences of his actions now startlingly clear. He was being blackmailed, but he dare not risk telling a living soul; he dare not risk the personal shame and the professional humiliation should his secret surface. How would he ever face his family and colleagues if the truth about what happened at that Interpol conference in Athens three years ago became public knowledge?

He would not be able to explain how that pretty little Romanian girl led him blindly from the bar to the bedroom and then, over the months that followed, deeper and deeper into a sordid world of group sex and on into drink and drug-fuelled orgies in lavish mansions across Europe.

And into the grip of the Hydra who, as he now knew, recorded it all with hidden video cameras, stills cameras and concealed microphones.

From a cupboard behind him, he produced an unopened bottle of Jameson's Irish whiskey and a Waterford crystal glass. By the time the bottle was one quarter empty, a plan had begun to form in his mind. By the time the bottle was half empty, the plan was complete and he could see, clear as day, that it offered him the only way out.

On his laptop he opened a new document and typed a letter to his wife. His fumbling fingers, constantly misdirected by his alcohol-addled brain, made continuous typing errors but he could not see them. He saw before him a statement of mitigation that could only have been crafted by a skilled and experienced lawyer. It ended with the words: 'I can only crave your forgiveness for the shame and humiliation I have heaped upon you.'

He printed it out and signed it with the looping hieroglyph that passed as his signature, sealed it into a CPS embossed envelope, scrawled his wife's name across the front and left it on his desk. Then he returned to the task of finishing the bottle of Jameson's.

He waited until the hub-bub of rush hour had subsided and the city had settled into its evening mantle. Below him hundreds of people were making their way to restaurants, to theatres, to bars with friends and families. It would be many hours before the crowds thinned out; many hours he could neither afford nor needed. He staggered out of his office and into the lift. At street level, he turned left and, barely able to stand, lurched his way northwards, towards Southwark Bridge itself. Ahead and to his left he could see the dome of St Paul's Cathedral, illuminated now in the gathering gloom. In his stupor, he bounced off several people, each time managing to mutter an apology that came out as 'Shhorr.'

At last he reached the middle of the bridge. He looked down over the parapet into the dark, murky waters of the River Thames, eddying around the bridge supports on an ebb tide. A convulsion gripped his stomach and he vomited. Virtually pure Irish whiskey cascaded from him into the water below. Seconds later he hauled himself onto the parapet and let go.

Even though it was early summer, the water temperature had barely crawled to 13°C. The shock of total cold water immersion increased his rate of breathing by eight times. Unable to control his breathing, he began to swallow water. The realisation of what he had done hit him. He didn't want to die. He tried to call out for help but succeeded only in swallowing even more water. He desperately tried to wave for help but couldn't raise his arms. Then, the panic rising within him triggered a massive cardiac arrest and he ceased breathing completely.

The RNLI's E-class lifeboat, blasted along by two huge outboard engines that gave it more power than a Formula One racing car, reached Southwark Bridge from its base on the Victoria embankment in under three minutes and the crew pulled Boulton from the water less than 10 minutes after he had entered it. But it was too late.

Cold water shock, the heart attack and the bottle of Jameson's had combined to ensure he would never have to face the humiliation he feared.

CHAPTER 14

Boulton's suicide only made a few paragraphs inside the following day's newspapers, largely because the Establishment closed ranks, partly in an attempt to spare his family the trauma of being door-stepped by hordes of reporters and partly because he had been an unturned stone. And no one was sure what now might crawl out from under it.

Scotland Yard disclosed nothing more than an RNLI lifeboat had recovered the body of a 45 year-old man from the River Thames close to Southwark Bridge. The RNLI confirmed the recovery but referred all other questions back to Scotland Yard. In Whitehall, the few enemies he had decided, independently, not to brief against him, leaving journalists to cobble together what they could from confused eye witnesses who could not agree on whether the man had fallen or had jumped. A couple of them said he had been 'behaving strangely' in the moments before the fall but none of them was aware that he was so drunk he would have been unfit to drive for days, not hours.

At the headquarters of the National Crime Agency, the feeling was that with Boulton dead there was a small sliver of light shining through what had previously been a tightly shuttered window.

By late morning, Bernard Copeland, Director of Border Policing, had convened a meeting in his office. Around the table sat his counterpart Michael Wilpshire, Director of the Organised Crime Command and agents Patrick Bird and Josh Sanford. Even though it had all been written down, encrypted, circulated to those who needed to see it and then carefully filed away, Bird and Sanford regurgitated every last scintilla they had gleaned from Cheryl Bonicki and from Robert Boulton himself.

'Agent Sanford and I are convinced that Mr Boulton's apparent suicide is directly linked to our visit to his office earlier yesterday,' said Bird. 'It was obvious he was hiding something or protecting someone or quite possibly both. He was in an extremely agitated state when we arrived and became quite aggressive. He flatly refused to answer any of our questions, especially as to why a man in his position would be so interested in a comparatively minor case. All he would say was that the CPS had decided prosecution of this chap Welbourne would not be in the public interest. We think Boulton and Welbourne are linked in some way.'

Copeland asked: 'Have your inquiries given you any indication of who it was he might have been trying to protect?'

'No sir. But whoever it was he was obviously very frightened of them to do what he did,' said Bird.

Sandford butted in. 'Mr Copeland, this is not a criticism, but we both felt that when we went to interview Mrs Bonicki and subsequently Mr Boulton, we hadn't been given the full facts. Is there something we should know?'

'Sorry Sandford, I'm not following you.'

'Well sir, to put it bluntly, neither of us could understand why we, the National Crime Agency, would be interested in the CPS dropping a relatively minor charge against a lorry driver who's as clean as a newly washed sheet. We both think there is more to this inquiry than we have been told.'

Copeland and Wilpshire exchanged concerned looks. Wilpshire rested his elbows on the table and began to massage his closed eyes with the heels of his hands.

'Go ahead Bernard,' he said from behind his hands. 'Tell them. Tell them about the operation.'

Copeland let out a long sigh which those closer to him would have recognised as an indication of reluctance. He thought for a few seconds and then said: 'Alright gentlemen, if you are going to be part of what looks like becoming a priority inquiry, you need to know the background. We — that is the NCA — are currently running an undercover operation to try to break an international crime syndicate, to which we have given the code name Hydra.

'This organisation is into drug smuggling, people smuggling, prostitution, gun-running, protection rackets. You name it, they do it. All over Europe and possibly even wider afield too. And they are able to continue to operate because, we believe, they have bought influence in high places, sometimes with straight forward bribery but usually with blackmail. The honey trap. It's the oldest trick in the book but it still works and only goes to prove how weak men are when they're confronted with a good-looking and obviously compliant young woman.'

Sandford was aware that his mouth was agape. 'So, are you saying that Boulton was being blackmailed by this Hydra? That they'd got something on him?'

'We believe so,' replied Copeland. 'It doesn't look like he consulted anybody else about dropping the charges against this Welbourne chap; he just did it off his own bat. And, as you said, why would he be interested in a case like that unless he was being put under pressure?'

'So where do we go from here?' asked Bird.

'I think we need to do some deep background on our Mr Boulton. I think he is key to leading us to the people behind the Hydra,' Copeland said. 'I want you two to concentrate on everything he has done, every case he's even thought about getting involved in, everywhere he's been and everyone he's met since he became Principal Legal Advisor. When we have that information, it will start opening doors.'

'And what about the undercover operation?' asked Bird.

'That will continue. You don't need to know the details and it's safer for those in the field if you don't. Now, I suggest you go and introduce yourselves to the Director of the Public Prosecutions. I'll get my secretary to make you an appointment. Oh, and one last thing — don't tell the DPP about the undercover operation. He doesn't need to know either at this stage.'

As the door closed behind the two by now bemused agents, Copeland turned to Wilpshire. 'D'you know Michael, I have a feeling that Colchester will prove to be just another cog in the gearbox. An important one admittedly, but I think we will find there's at least one other even bigger one.'

'So what are we going to do with Wilson?'

'Nothing. We leave him in situ. But I need to get a message to him about Boulton and get him to see what he can come up with by way of records; anything that's written down or recorded in any way. I think Boulton's suicide could be the beginning of the end for Hydra.'

***

This time it was Jan who instituted the meeting, choosing once again the Goat and Boot as the venue. She found Ray standing at the bar, half way down a pint, and gave him a light peck on the cheek. He bought her a pint and a second one for himself before they sat down in a quiet corner, which was not difficult to find so early in the evening.

'There's been a significant development you need to be aware of,' said Jan after their brief exchange of pleasantries. 'A guy at the top of the CPS has topped himself and the powers that be think it's linked to your charges being dropped.'

'What? How? I mean...who was this guy and what's the link?'

'He was called Robert Boulton and he was Principal Legal Advisor, just one down from the DPP herself,' Jan explained. 'He was the one who leaned on CPS Eastern Region to drop the charges against you and Pilling Transport. With the information and photographs you supplied from Pillings, our people recognised interference, probably from Hydra. Two of their guys went to interview the head of CPS Eastern and as a result of that went to speak to Boulton. Apparently he was very uncooperative. But when they'd gone, he swallowed a whole bottle of whiskey and chucked himself into the Thames.'

'Bit drastic. Unless he had a whole lot to hide.'

'That's just it,' Jan said. 'Our people believe he was being blackmailed by Hydra. The two guys who went to interview him are currently on a deep background investigation, finding out every dot and comma about him. They're convinced that if they can find out why he was being blackmailed, it will open doors for the investigation.

'In the meantime, you stay in place but they want you to search for any records of any kind that might help establish a link, no matter how tenuous, between Boulton and Hydra — or between them and anybody else in high office come to that. They're getting very excited. They think this is the break they've been waiting for.'

'I'll do what I can, but to be honest I don't have a clue where to start looking,' Ray said. 'And, of course, the opportunities are somewhat limited. Now, do you fancy another drink or shall we go for a bite to eat?'

'Neither I'm afraid. I've got someone to meet,' she said, draining her drink.

Touché, he thought.

CHAPTER 15

Night had shrouded the sky with a thick covering of cloud, through which not even the tiniest pinprick of starlight could penetrate. A brisk north easterly breeze had picked up the North Sea and created a short chop of two-metre waves, which made for an uncomfortable passage for anyone out there in a small boat.

But on board the UK Border Force's cutter Vigilant, the sea state could hardly be felt. At 140 feet long and powered by two diesel electric engines capable of pushing her along at 26 knots, the waves posed no issue for the 16-man crew. And although the bridge bristled with electronic technology that gave her eyes and ears in the dark, a watch was still maintained by two men equipped with night-vision binoculars.

It was one of these men who saw the little dark-hulled fishing boat first. She was a couple of miles away on the port side, sailing towards the Essex coast in the opposite direction to Vigilant, head-on to the weather. The sighting would have been unremarkable, were it not for the fact that the boat was not showing any navigation lights, in breach of maritime regulations. It was a favourite trick of smugglers attempting to avoid detection and therefore immediately aroused suspicion.

'I've got a small boat to port not showing any nav lights, sir,' the watchman reported to the Officer of the Watch. 'It's heading approximately west south west.'

'Thank you Samms. Keep an eye on her and I'll hail her,' the officer replied.

He picked up the microphone for the VHF radio that was kept permanently tuned to Channel 16, the international distress and hailing frequency used by mariners around the world. He pressed the transmit button and said: 'Small vessel on my port side, bearing 030, this is UK Border Force Cutter Vigilant. Please identify yourself. I say again. Vessel bearing 030 from my position, this is Border Force Cutter Vigilant. Please identify yourself. Over.'

At first there was no response and he was just about to make a second hail when the radio crackled. 'Cutter Vigilant, Cutter Vigilant, Cutter

Vigilant,' said a disembodied voice, 'this is the fishing boat Serendipity. Serendipity, over.'

'Serendipity, can you explain why you aren't showing any navigation lights?'

A brief pause and then. 'Er..No. They were on. They must have got knocked out. We'll take a look at them. Thank you for telling us. Over.'

Before he made a response, the officer turned to his watchman. 'Samms, tell me what you can see on board Serendipity.'

'Nothing sir,' Samms replied. 'There's no one in the wheelhouse and there's no sign of life anywhere else.'

'Well, someone's using the radio. Let's take a closer look.'

Over the radio, the officer said: 'Serendipity, I'm not satisfied with that response. Heave to and prepare for a boarding party. Vigilant out; standing by on Channel 16.'

Then he picked up another microphone and made a Tannoy announcement. 'RIB crew to launch stations. RIB crew to launch stations. We have a suspicious vessel, bearing 030.'

Within minutes, the five-man crew of the rigid inflatable were on board their boat and preparing to launch down the specially constructed slipway at the stern of the cutter. As they were entering the water, the starboard lookout on the bridge also spotted something suspicious through his night-vision binoculars.

'Sir, there's what appears to be a pleasure craft about four miles ahead. She's just turned off her nav-lights and done a 180 degree turn,' he reported. 'Looks like she's heading for the Dutch coast.'

'OK. Alert the Dutch Coastguard. We'll sort them out later.'

Vigilant had closed to within 200 yards of the boat that claimed to be the Serendipity and trained powerful searchlights on the vessel, which was drifting without power. Despite the brilliance of the light, no one appeared on deck and no one answered the repeated calls from the RIB. It was as if the small craft had been abandoned.

Hidden in the darkness, a 45-foot cabin cruiser thundered towards the sanctuary of Vlissingen's huge harbour.

With no power and at the mercy of the sea and the wind, Serendipity was pitching wildly as the Border Force RIB closed on her port side, using the wind, which was increasing in ferocity, to take her and hold her alongside. It took all the helmsman's skill to manoeuvre the RIB into a position from which the crew could heave a grappling iron over the fishing boat's rail and secure it. Seconds later, three men stood on the deck and the RIB stood off at a safe distance, leaving the grappling iron in place.

Dressed in black from head to toe, the three Border Force officers could easily have been mistaken for special forces soldiers, although they were unarmed and carried only torches. A quick sweep of the deck revealed an absence of fishing gear of any kind. The small wheelhouse at the back of boat was deserted. The lightening search — primarily for people on board — missed the rectangular black box fastened to the instrument panel and it would be many hours before its existence was noted and several more before its purpose was revealed.

The hatch immediately in front of the wheelhouse had been secured by a steel bar. Two of the men removed it and lifted the hatch cover allowing an unexpected loom of red light to escape. One of them lowered his head through the hatch and swept the space with his torch.

'Jesus Charlie, it's full of women,' he yelled.

'Yeah, right. Always full of shit aren't you Jimmy?' Charlie replied.

'Seriously. It is. Have a look'

Charlie stuck his head into the space. His nose was assaulted by the stench of vomit mixed with urine and diesel fumes but in the red gloom he could see a number of figures, most of them lying in pipe cots, some of them retching. The cabin floor was awash with sick and urine from the blocked sea toilet in its three-sided steel cage. A sweep of his torch revealed 12 women, all of them in their late teens or early 20s.

'Christ. What the hell is going on?' he said out loud to no one in particular. Then he shouted: 'Pete, call Vigilant and say we've got 12 women in the hold. Some of them look in a pretty bad way.'

He and Jimmy then climbed into the hold, to be greeted by screams, terrified eyes and a babble of shouted words in a language he did not understand that could have been curses, questions, prayers or a mixture of all three. But the one thing he did understand was that these women were frightened; frightened for their very lives and frightened of him.

Charlie made a soothing motion with his hands. 'It's alright ladies. Just stay calm. We're not going to hurt you,' he said. 'We're from the UK Border Force. We're going to get you out of here and take you somewhere safe.'

One of the women began to translate and the aura of fear began to dissipate.

'Do you speak English?' he asked the woman, who now sat on the edge of her pipe cot, clutching a small, cheap plastic holdall, her head covered by a bright green scarf.

'A little. Enough I think,' she replied.

'Good, good,' Charlie said. 'Tell them that we have a ship and we're going to move you all on to that. Tell them there's nothing to worry about.'

'Where are you taking us?' the woman asked, eyes wide.

'We'll land in England. At our base in Kent. A place called Gravesend.'

'Will we be allowed stay there?'

'I don't know. I can't make any promises.'

'But we must stay. We have paid much money.'

'Let's not worry about that right now. We need to get you to safety.'

While the woman was translating his words for her fellow travellers, Pete came down the short companionway.

'The Boss says get them on deck and he'll bring Vigilant alongside. We should be able to do a straight transfer without too many problems,' he said.

Charlie turned to his translator. 'My name's Charlie. What's yours?'

'Louka. My name is Louka,' she said.

'And where are you from?'

'I am coming from Chechnya. I go to England to make new life.'

Charlie sighed inwardly. He knew the chances of that were less then remote. 'OK Louka, I need you to tell your companions what's going to happen right now.'

Twenty minutes later, the twelve women had been transferred safely to Vigilant and were being fed in the cutter's crew mess. Two of them had been placed in the sick bay and put on saline drips to combat the dehydration brought on by severe sea-sickness.

Serendipity was taken in tow, Jimmy and Pete remaining on board to steer her, and Vigilant made a course towards Gravesend and home.

With several miles to run in to Vlissingen harbour, the cabin cruiser turned its navigation lights back on and continued its voyage home. On board, the atmosphere amongst the four crewmen was becoming less tense. Ever since the Border Force cutter had discovered the radio-controlled fishing boat, anxiety levels had been running high, but now that the boat was well into the River Scheldt and probably less than an hour from her berth, the four believed they could relax.

The tops were cracked from four bottles of beer, which were raised simultaneously in salute. They had lost the fishing boat but lived to smuggle another day.

It was at the exact moment that the cruiser was bathed in brilliant white light as a Dutch Coastguard cutter loomed out of the darkness and a booming loudspeaker announcement ordered them to heave to. In less than a minute a powerful RIB had pulled alongside, manned by armed police from the Royal Marechaussee, the branch of the National Police Corps charged with guarding Holland's borders.

The salutations paled. And the beer went unconsumed.

When Vigilant arrived in Gravesend, the two sick women were taken to the local hospital for further treatment and observation while the remaining ten were transferred to the immigrant detention centre in Dover to await their fate. The trawler Serendipity was put into a safe berth to await the attentions of expert investigators.

At around the same time that office workers in Gravesend were booting up computers and making the first coffee of the day, two Border Force inspectors were climbing aboard Serendipity. The only clue to their identity was the large lettering on the backs of their bright yellow hi-viz vests. Both men carried clip-boards and torches and it took them only a few seconds to spot something that was out of place.

Brian Hennessy had spent most of his working life as an engineer in the Merchant Navy, starting as a 16 year-old apprentice and retiring 40 years later as Chief Engineer in a 125,000 tonne bulk carrier. He had never seen anything like the device he was now staring at in the trawler's wheelhouse. Fastened to the small, simple instrument panel, immediately alongside the dials that showed engine revs, oil pressure and fuel level was a black rectangular box.

'Billy, come and have a look at this,' he called to his companion. 'I haven't got a clue what it's for.'

Billy Middleton was also an ex-Merchant Navy engineer. Born and raised in Co Cork, he had moved to Liverpool in his early teens but had served in so many ships with so many men of different nationalities he now spoke with a thousand accents and with none.

He examined the box from every angle, tried to lift it, prodded it and stroked it. Then he shone his torch under the instrument panel and spotted the loom of wires that disappeared beneath the wheelhouse floor.

'It's an odd looking thing for sure,' he declared. 'But I'm fucked if I know what it does. Better get one of the electronics boys to come and have a look. There's a shit-load of wires coming from it. Maybe it's a new sort of auto-helm. But I'm guessing.'

Hennessy made a call on his mobile phone and then the pair of them set about combing through the rest of the boat while they waited for the electronics man. What they found left them in no doubt that the true purpose of Serendipity was as far removed from fishing as it was possible to get.

There were no nets, no baskets, no fish storage space, no marker buoys, none of the paraphernalia that would be expected on even the smallest in-shore fishing vessel. Instead, what should have been the hold where the day's catch was kept had been converted. It was now a large open space with 12 pipe cots — lengths of tough canvas stretched over aluminium tubing — screwed to the walls, six down each side in two rows of three, one above the other. Two bulkhead lights gave out a dim red glow and in the bow was a sea toilet contained in an open sided steel cage. The fact that it was blocked and out of service was evidenced by the stink that permeated the area.

Hennessy was struck by the thought that the stench of urine, vomit, sweat and stale diesel fumes was the reek of broken dreams, the odour of abandoned hope. Both men were left in no doubt that the true current purpose of Serendipity, irrespective of when, where and why she was built, was now smuggling. Smuggling people.

A couple of hours had passed by the time Jack Partridge arrived. Partridge was in his mid thirties and was known to his colleagues as "The Professor" because of his MSc in electronic engineering. He too wore a Border Force hi-viz vest but instead of a clipboard, he carried a hard-case crammed with tools with which he could take apart and reassemble any kind of electronic instrument. He was well-known to both Hennessy and Middleton.

'Good morning gentlemen. What appears to be the problem?' he asked casually.

'It's this thing,' replied Middleton, pointing into the wheelhouse. 'Neither of us knows what it is, although it's connected to something below deck. We think it might be some kind of fancy auto-helm.'

'OK. Let's take a look.'

He stepped into the wheelhouse, put his tool kit on the floor, took one look at the black box and asked: 'Was this boat under command when she was intercepted?'

'No. One of the guys who went aboard told me there were only 12 women and they were locked in the hold,' Hennessy said. 'There was no one in the wheelhouse.'

'I didn't think so,' Partridge said. 'You were right Billy when you said it could be some kind of fancy auto-helm. This thing is an APM 2.6 control board. It's built for amateur use but it's basically the same technology that they use in aerial drones.

'The boat was being radio-controlled.'

'What? A boat this big? You're taking the piss,' Middleton said.

'No, I'm serious. Give me an hour or two and I'll tell you exactly how it was done. Go and have a coffee. I'll ring you when I've finished.'

It was early afternoon by the time Brian Hennessy's mobile rang and the two engineers returned to the berth where Serendipity was moored. Partridge was leaning on the rail with a triumphant expression on his face.

'Gentlemen, I have to say that whoever put this kit together knew exactly what they were doing,' he said. 'I'm impressed. And I'd say this wasn't the first one they've done. There could be other radio-controlled vessels out there.'

From his tool box he produced a hand-drawn wiring diagram which he spread out on the boat's small chart table.

'This is how it works,' he began. 'As I said the APM 2.6 control board is for amateur use but it's designed to be highly configurable. It comes with open source mission planning software that can be accessed in real time via a sat-phone or radio to change waypoints, view sensor values yadda-yadda...

'In this boat, it's connected to the GPS, depth sounder, compass and autopilot using NMEA strings that come with the kit. It can output signals to the rudder and it has a series of solenoids to operate the throttle and control speed. It's quite capable of navigating itself to within a few metres of waypoints set in the planning software, although, as I've said, those waypoints can be adjusted in real time using radio telemetry from anything up to 20 miles away.

'It's also got fore and aft video transmitters so that whoever is controlling it can get a good look around. All-in-all, it's pretty sophisticated.'

Hennessy and Middleton looked at each mystified. Partridge may just as well have spoken to them in Swahili. But they understood the gist of what he had said and the threat it posed.

'How close would someone need to be to control it?' asked Hennessy.

'The radio telemetry module that allows you to view data such as depth, engine speed etc has a range of about six miles. You could do it very easily off a beach or a headland. Or you could do it from another boat following that far behind.'

'Interesting,' Middleton said. 'Vigilant reported seeing a cabin cruiser about four miles behind when she intercepted this thing. The cruiser turned off its nav lights and did a 180 back towards Holland. Apparently the Dutch Coastguard arrested it as it approached Vlissingen.'

An indulgent smile crossed Partridge's face. 'That's exactly the kind of thing I'm talking about.'

The three men shook hands and said their goodbyes. Hennessy and Middleton returned to their office to write their report. And to alert their bosses to the new threat that had been discovered.

CHAPTER 16

Even though it was almost dark and outside the air had a distinct chill, Ray could feel the beads of sweat running down his spine. This was a dangerous game he was playing. If he was discovered, it would be over and Pilling would take delight in drawing out his death in as painful a manner as he could think of over as long a period as possible.

Tasked by his masters to find whatever he could that was filed away, written down or otherwise stored, Ray had been forced to take a gamble, staking his own safety on the fact that there would be no one at the depot — and that no one would return to it at that time of night.

But even though he stood a good chance of getting away with it this time, he knew that it was impossible to conduct a thorough search on his own. He would have to do it all over again. And again and again until he had either found what he was looking for or had exhausted all possibilities. Each time the odds on discovery would increase.

He had set up tonight's adventure by ringing Summer on his way back from Birmingham claiming he was stuck in a traffic tail-back caused by an accident on the motorway. He had asked to her make sure the gates were left unlocked so he could return the van. He also asked her to leave a key so he could lock up and text him to say where she had hidden it. In fact, when he made the call he was at a transport cafe only half an hour's drive from the depot, so he had settled down for almost two hours to be certain the place would be deserted when he arrived.

He got there to find that Summer had done as he'd asked; the gates yielded to his touch and a text message told him where the key for the huge padlock was hidden. It was a precaution aimed at not arousing the girl's suspicions because in the small rucksack he had taken to carrying everywhere was his duplicate set of keys.

Ray parked the van, recovered the hidden padlock key and then let himself into the offices, which he had decided was the most likely place to find any incriminating evidence.

He sat at Mike Pilling's desk, systematically going through the drawers, none of which was locked. He started at the bottom and worked upwards, revealing nothing more than that most of them were empty.

One contained a clutch of old copies of the trade magazine Commercial Motor and two unused A4 notepads. Another was a jumble of odds and ends: a stapler, a pair of scissors, a plastic ruler, cheap branded key rings and a couple of bottle openers. He had even removed each drawer to check whether anything had been taped to the outside of them. It hadn't. Then he examined underneath the desk to see if anything had been concealed there. It hadn't.

He casually opened the lid of Pilling's Dell laptop and tapped the "on" button, fully expecting entry to be barred by a password. To his surprise, the machine whirred into life, apparently completely unprotected. Ray's knowledge of computers was limited but he recognised that the laptop was using the Windows Vista operating system. Across the top of the screen was the Dell Dock, which displayed an array of icons that were shortcuts to the user's favourite programmes. He clicked on the e-mail and watched as Windows Mail opened to view.

A quick scan down the inbox showed nothing more than messages from Pilling's real-world customers, some of them asking for quotes for particular jobs, some giving delivery instructions and a couple complaining about the service they had received. He checked the sent messages but they too revealed nothing untoward.

One thing Ray did know about Windows Mail was that its address book was filled from a separate programme called Windows Contacts. He clicked on the Start button, then on All Programmes and scrolled down until he found what he was looking for. From his rucksack he produced a 512kb memory stick and seconds later he had a copy of every e-mail address the programme held.

He turned his attention to the bank of four steel filing cabinets, each four drawers high, which flanked one wall. Again, none of them was locked but more than an hour fine-tooth-combing the contents disclosed nothing that would link Pilling, his business or any of his employees to Hydra.

If any such evidence existed, it wasn't in the boss's office.

By now the falling of night was complete and he recognised the risk of continuing to work — any chink of light could attract the attention of a passing police patrol or, worse, from some nosy bastard who knew Mike Pilling. It was time to call it a day.

***

The following day, a Saturday, he slipped through the gates not long after eight-thirty in the morning, determined to give himself as much time as possible to continue his search. If he was found, he would have to rely on the old lost-wallet-in-the van excuse and the fact that he had used the key left for him by Summer.

This time he began in the building he had come to know as "Mike's Shed," in which he had discovered the crude dormitory, the photographic studio and the pictures of Anna. He stared at the three cars under their dust covers, apparently undisturbed since his last visit. They would make a good hiding place but a pretty obvious one. He decided they would be his last resort and climbed the wooden staircase towards the dormitory.

Inside, the rows of bunks were still there but stripped of their meagre bedding. The bins were empty, the kitchen area and small bathroom reasonably clean. He spent a few minutes going through the limited storage spaces, under the sink, in the single kitchen cupboard and in the bathroom. Nothing. He sat on the edge of a bunk and stared around him, praying for inspiration. But none came. Eventually he decided this was not the place to hide anything and turned his attention to the row of four office rooms downstairs.

Like the last time he was here, three of them were empty but he still gave them the once-over, searching for anything that might be concealed there. Apart from a couple of very large spiders —which scuttled off and dived between floorboards at his approach — and a lot of dust, his search was fruitless.

He stood outside the end office, the one he knew to be a photographic studio, leafing through his bunch of duplicate keys, guessing which one would let him in. He got it at the second attempt. Everything was exactly as he remembered it. The roll of white back-drop paper still hung on the wall. The two powerful studio flashes were still trained on it and in the centre the Nikon D4 was still fixed to its tripod.

This time Ray concentrated his efforts on the filing cabinets and drawers that stood along the back wall, unseeing, unspeaking witnesses to the humiliations piled upon girls who genuinely believed they were on the threshold of a new and prosperous life.

Yet again he discovered that most of them were empty. One filing cabinet drawer contained several boxes of photographic printing paper and another was full of bottles of chemicals, throw-backs to an era when producing photographs was a skilled and time-consuming process.

In a third drawer he found a stack of black and white prints, each showing hopeful young women naked, forced smiles on their faces, in poses that left absolutely nothing to the imagination and could be best described as gynaecological. Their existence reinforced to Ray just how long the Hydra had been in business.

Again, he spent time meticulously removing each drawer and checking for anything taped to its outside. Again, there was nothing.

In the corner was a cheap wooden desk that looked like it had come from one of the many flat-pack specialist companies. It had three drawers, which were also empty, an office chair and a laptop. Ray slumped into the chair, opened the laptop and pushed the "on" button, more in hope than expectation. This time his hope was dashed. The computer demanded a password.

His sigh would have been audible if there had been anybody around to hear it. He had a stab at one, then another and another and another, all of which were rejected. He was just about to give up when, with an inspiration he would never be able to explain, he typed: "all_ie_summer". To his amazement the laptop screen opened up before him and he found himself staring at a screen-saver that was a close-up of Summer's face. On the desktop were a series of files identified only by date. He clicked on the first one which opened to reveal more than 100 numbered thumbnail icons. He clicked at random on the icon closest to the cursor.

It filled the screen with an image that made Ray's eyes open wide in disbelief. The picture showed Summer lying on a sofa, naked apart from a pair of white stilettos. She was having sex. With Mike Pilling.

The other images in the file completed a series that began with Summer fully clothed and ended when Pilling had climaxed. All the other files were identical, the only difference being in what Summer was wearing, what she removed and what she kept on.

He rocked back in the chair, stunned at what the laptop had revealed. It was a pairing he would never have imagined, even in his wildest dreams, but he now realised that whatever he said to Summer would be reported directly to Pilling. Summer might not be part of Hydra but she was close — very close — to its boss. It was information that might prove useful but it was also information that would make him think twice before he said anything to her that was even remotely critical or controversial.

Ray closed down the computer and pushed the chair away from the desk. As he did so, he felt the tilt as a castor caught on something below the nylon rug under his feet. He rolled the rug away to find that a section of floorboard, probably no more than four inches long, had been sawn through. He pressed one end and the section lifted easily to reveal a small plastic box, the kind that cheap jewellers use to package cheap ear-rings. He opened it.

Inside was a 32GB micro-sd memory card.

He swiftly removed the micro-sd card from his mobile and inserted the one he had found. A dialogue box told him his phone did not have enough memory to complete the task so he took a gamble. He slipped the phone with the 32GB card still in it, back in his pocket and put the empty plastic box back in its hiding place.

Half an hour later he was in an electronics store in Colchester where he bought an adaptor for £10 and a 32GB USB drive for £25.

Back at his flat, he poured himself a beer, inserted the micro-sd card and its adaptor in his laptop and opened it.

He found photographs, lots of photographs, of men with girls, many of them barely out of their teens, in positions that the red-top tabloids would take delight in describing as compromising. A lot of the images appeared to have been taken in hotel bedrooms but most of them had been taken in the same room, a room with a circular bed, red flock wallpaper and a level of lighting just sufficient to allow the concealed camera to take an identifiable picture. He had little doubt that the girls had been gleaned from the pathetic cargoes that the Hydra specialised in smuggling into the UK.

Ray padded over to the fridge and poured himself a second beer.

He estimated that the memory card held close to 10,000 images but he had neither the time nor the taste to examine them all, so he contended himself with a quick scan through the first 50 or so. In doing so he identified two men he knew to be Members of Parliament, one who was the editor of a national newspaper, a well-known TV presenter and another who was a QC and judge.

He knew that what he was looking at was the mother-lode; the honey-trap in all its pitiable glory; the flesh of man rendered vulnerable by the lure of sexual promise. It was dynamite. The mere existence of these photographs was enough to destroy hundreds of careers, ruin countless lives, rip apart innocent families.

And put each and every one of these men at the mercy of the Hydra.

Ray swallowed the dregs of his beer, inserted the 32GB flash drive and carefully copied every image from the micro memory card. It would be for others to trawl through them, putting names and occupations to as many faces as possible, a task that would finally reveal the true extent of the Hydra's reach.

When the copying was complete, he took the flash drive into the bathroom where he prised open the bath panel just enough to get his fingers inside, dropped the now priceless piece of plastic behind it and hammered the panel back with the palm of his hand.

He put the micro memory card back in his phone and rang Jan. Unusually it went straight to voicemail so he left a message, trying desperately to sound light-hearted while at the same time underlining the urgency with which he needed to speak to her.

Then a third beer seemed the right thing to do.

***

Ray awoke with a start at the urgent jangling sound his brain had recognised as the ring tone of his mobile phone. Outside darkness had fallen and the flickering of the television in the corner provided the only light. In his partially wakened state he groped to find his phone and succeeded only in knocking over his half empty beer glass. He cursed but then spotted the light of his phone's screen underneath that day's Daily Telegraph. It was Jan.

'Hi. You wanted me.' It was a statement rather than a question. 'Sorry, I was in the bath when you rang and I must have fallen asleep. I look like a giant pink prune.'

It was an image Ray struggled to reconcile with the Jan he knew and the totally professional policewoman he admired. Nonetheless his response was brief and to the point: 'Yeah. Thanks for calling back. Shall we go out for lunch tomorrow?'

'Er... yeah okay. Where do you fancy?' He recognised the hesitation in her voice and knew at once that he was still not completely forgiven.

'I don't have anywhere in mind,' he said. 'Somewhere out of town I think. I'll see what I can find. Pick you up about eleven-thirty?'

'Okay. See you then.' And she was gone.

***

By seven-thirty the following morning, Ray was easing his way into Pilling's depot. He had parked the battered BMW in a lay by about quarter of a mile away, not wanting to leave it on show in the yard. Using his duplicate keys, he opened the office, went through to "Mike's Shed" and opened the photographic dark room. It took him less than a minute to find the under-floor hiding place, open it and replace the 32GB micro memory card. Ten minutes later he was back in his car and heading back to the flat.

Jan appeared as soon as the car came to a stop outside her flat. As she walked down the path towards him, dressed in designer jeans and a white linen shirt with a navy blue, fern-patterned scarf knotted loosely around her neck, Ray realised that despite the messages he may have given out, he did find her attractive. But as casual and cosy as they may have seemed to others, their relationship was — and would stay — purely professional.

She climbed into the passenger seat, leaned over and gave him a peck on the cheek, this time without the 'That's just for appearances' rider.

'Where are we off to then?' she asked as the car pulled away from the kerb.

'There's a place called The Anchor in Nayland, not far away,' he said. 'It seems to be very popular. I've been on the website and the food looks great.'

For several minutes Jan stared silently out of the car window. Then: 'I assume that all this is because you have something for me and not simply because you enjoy my sparkling company.'

Without taking his eyes from the road, Ray replied: 'Detective Inspector Holroyd, you do yourself a disservice. I've always found you to be charming and entertaining to be around. That's one of the reasons why I asked for you as my liaison. And yes, I have got something for you; something major this time. If I hadn't wanted to spend some time with you I could just have easily handed it over on the pavement and left.'

'I have to say that's not the impression you gave me the other night when you were round at mine.'

'Jan, let's not go there,' he said. 'We both know why that won't work so let's just agree to stay as good friends and get this bloody job done and dusted.'

There was a mumbled 'Okay,' from the passenger seat, followed by a more audible: 'So, what you have got that's so great?'

As they drove, he told her about finding the 32GB memory card and described what was on the few images he had looked at.

'I reckon there's probably close to ten thousand pictures on it,' he said. 'It's going to need somebody — actually probably a few people — to go through every image and identify all the men in them. It's going to be a ball-ache, but it will give us a bloody good idea of just how high up the ladder of authority the Hydra's domination reaches.

'I also got a look at Mike Pilling's laptop but it wasn't very forthcoming. I managed to copy his e-mail address book but, to be honest, it's not going to be much use. It's work related stuff. I doubt there will be anything of interest on it.'

When they reached The Anchor Ray gave Jan the two flash drives.

'I suggest you get these to Wilpshire and co as quickly as possible. Like I said, it's going to be a big job going through those pictures.'

'I appreciate that,' she replied. 'I plan on taking them into London myself tomorrow. I'll get an early train.'

Inside The Anchor, they both opted for traditional Sunday lunch — sirloin of beef with Yorkshire pudding, roast potatoes and all the trimmings. Ray ordered a pint of Adnams Southwold bitter. Jan thought about ordering the same but settled for a half instead.

As they ate, she asked Ray: 'You said you'd copied Pilling's address book to this little flash drive. What e-mail programme was he running?'

'Windows Mail. Why?'

'Well, I don't know whether you know this but he could also be running another e-mail programme alongside it,' she said. 'Like, if he's got Microsoft Office 2007 or later, he'll have Outlook as part of that package. It doesn't have to show in the desktop. How did you find Windows Mail?'

'I could see his laptop was running Windows Vista as the operating system. It's the same as mine so I knew he would have Windows Mail and I knew where to look for the contacts book.'

'Have you not got Outlook on yours then?'

'I've no idea. You know me and technology; I'm something of an anti-Christ when it comes to gadgets. I just about know the basics. So assuming I do get another chance to look at his laptop, where would I find this Outlook?'

Jan took a swig of beer. 'You'd need to go to the start menu, then click on All Programmes, then look for Microsoft Office...'

She saw Ray's eyes glaze over. She knew he wanted the information but he was only pretending to follow what she was saying.

'...I tell you what, when you get a chance to get into his laptop again, ring me and I'll talk you through what you need to do.'

The rest of lunch passed in a fug of small talk, shared jokes about the people they had left behind in Bradford; anything but work.

Back in the car and heading once again for Colchester, Ray suddenly said: 'I've had an idea. Why don't we go and look at Pilling's laptop now?'

'What? Right now?' Jan was taken aback at the suggestion. 'Will it be safe? I mean, what if we get caught?'

'We won't,' Ray said, with more than a touch of bravado. 'It's Sunday afternoon. There'll be nobody there. And if there is, you're my girlfriend and we've just come to see if I've dropped my wallet in the van. It's the excuse I've always had in my head but I haven't had to use it yet.'

'Okay, if you're sure.'

'We won't get a better chance. You know what you're doing with this Outlook thing; you're with me now and you're going to London tomorrow. It's a perfect fit.'

Twenty minutes later, the BMW was parked in the lay-by for the second time that day. As they had driven past the depot, the colour had drained from Jan's face. 'Christ Ray, there's more CCTV cameras here than at Buckingham Palace. We're bound to get seen.'

'Don't worry,' he said. 'They're only trained on the outside of the perimeter fence and anyway, Summer told me they don't work anymore and Pilling won't pay for them to be repaired.'

'Summer?' Jan said with a fake note of amazement. 'Who the fuck's Summer?'

'She's Mike Pilling's secretary,' Mike replied 'and from what I found in the studio yesterday she's his amateur co-porn star too.'

'Well, she's certainly got the name for it,' Jan said.

'Oh, it gets better. Her surname's Long.'

Jan convulsed with laughter. 'Summer Long? Summer Long? I think Summer-one was taking the piss when they named her. Why doesn't the stupid cow change it?'

'She says she daren't while her parents are alive. They've always told her it's the most beautiful name in the world.'

'Fucking hell. If there was ever a case in favour of justifiable homicide, I think Summer Long is it.'

By then they were inside the office block and Ray was opening up Pilling's laptop.

'There you are. All yours,' he said standing.

It took Jan less than a minute to find Outlook and open the address book.

It contained just eleven addresses.

Ray handed her another 512kb flash drive and with a few deft key strokes she copied the lot. Then, as an after-thought, she clicked a couple more times and revealed the e-mail address that Pilling used with the Outlook account. That too went on to the flash drive.

'Right, let's get out of here. This place gives me the creeps,' she said.

It wasn't until they were safely back on the road home that she spoke again. 'Fancy another drink?' she asked.

Ray took the question as an indication that diplomatic relations had been re-established. He didn't answer but gave her an inquisitory glance.

'We can either find a pub or I've got a few bottles of Duval and a nice bottle of sauvignon blanc in the fridge. No strings. Promise.'

Ray looked in his rear-view mirror, indicated a right turn and made the manoeuvre that would take them to her front door.

CHAPTER 17

The following morning Jan squashed herself on to the 7.42am to London's Liverpool Street Station. Like every other morning, the train was crammed to capacity with commuters, all busily avoiding making eye contact with their fellow travellers and pretending to be engrossed in something or other. Those lucky enough to have a seat had their noses buried in a newspaper or a novel; some found fascination in their mobile phones. Those who were condemned to stand either stared blankly into space or listened to music on tiny, tinnie earphones connected to unseen gadgets.

Jan carried a large, ostentatious, but fake, Mulberry handbag, which she kept clutched to her as if it contained all the secrets of her life. In fact it contained nothing more than her make-up bag, a telescopic umbrella and a bottle of water. Its primary purposed was for jabbing into the kidneys of commuters who unwisely encroached on what she considered to be her personal space.

The three precious flash drives were concealed in a slim money belt that she wore next to her skin, beneath her black, baggy trousers.

In just over an hour, her ordeal by train was over and she, along with what seemed like half the population of Essex was vomited from the station's vast interior onto the street from which it takes its name. She had toyed with getting straight onto the Underground but her journey overground had caused her sufficient angst that it took only a millisecond to opt for a taxi to complete her journey to the National Crime Agency's headquarters.

When she arrived, neither of the two men she had travelled to see had any notion of her visit so she was obliged to wait for over an hour while diaries were hastily rearranged to accommodate her. Eventually she was ushered into the office of Bernard Copeland, Director of Border Policing, and found him already seated at the meeting table with Michael Wilpshire, Director of the Organised Crime Command, on his right hand side. Behind them on top of a solid oak cabinet were two pump-action flasks, one containing freshly made coffee and the other boiling hot water to make tea. Copeland insisted on dispensing drinks as a prelude to business.

The cup of black coffee stood on the table untouched as she took the flash drives — which she had retrieved from their hiding place while waiting for the meeting to begin — from her handbag. She clutched them in her left hand. 'Gentlemen,' she began, 'I think Ray may have struck gold.'

She carefully and deliberately placed the first flash drive on the table in front of her.

'This contains all the e-mail addresses from Mike Pilling's laptop.'

She placed the second drive alongside the first.

'This one contains all the e-mail addresses from a secret e-mail account Pilling runs from the same laptop.'

Finally, she put down the 32GB drive.

'And this, gentlemen, contains literally thousands of photographs of men in compromising positions with young women. When you see them, you may well think that it's from these images that the Hydra derives the power it seems to wield over the Establishment.'

Jan sat back and picked up the coffee, watching with inner amusement as the incredulity spread across the faces of the two men opposite her.

'This is amazing,' said Wilpshire. 'How on earth has Wilson managed to get his hands on this stuff? Potentially it's explosive.'

'I don't know. Ray hasn't told me and I haven't asked,' Jan lied. 'We thought it better for security if I didn't know.'

Copeland said: 'Give Wilson our sincere thanks next time you see him. We'll need to get all this information analysed and the photographs identified, of course, but I think we might be rapidly approaching the point where we can start cutting off the Hydra's heads.'

Jan smiled as she put the coffee cup back on the desk. 'But as I remember it,' she began, recalling something Ray had told her, 'when one of the Hydra's nine heads was cut off, it grew two more in its place.'

'You're perfectly right Inspector Holroyd,' Copeland answered. 'It was also said that one of the heads was immortal. But Hercules found a way to kill the beast and so shall we. And that task will be accomplished in no small measure because of the information you have brought us today.

'Wilson needs to tread very carefully now. Once we begin to act on this information, he could find himself compromised. I'm sure he's aware of that but please reinforce it to him. We want him back safely when all this is over.'

'Rest assured I will pass on your regards and your concerns sir, but I know DCI Wilson is very conscious of his current position and the threat he faces,' said Jan.

'Thank you Inspector Holroyd,' said Copeland. 'And now if you will excuse us, we have some serious organising to do to evaluate what we have here as speedily and as accurately as possible.'

***

An hour later, Jan found herself on a return train to Colchester but this time, apart from a pair of pensioners and a young woman with a baby, she was alone in the carriage. She had plenty of time to reflect on the increased risks that Ray now faced. She had no doubt that the NCA would now seek authorisation to hack into all the e-mail traffic from Pilling's address books, the business ones as well as the secret ones. They would also tap his mobile and landlines.

But the real danger would come when they started to identify the men in the photographs. It would undoubtedly take more than one person to carry out that exercise. And the more people who knew, the greater the chance of a leak. It could be an accidental leak or a deliberate one, but the outcome would be the same. Ray's life would be in jeopardy.

Jan was also acutely aware that there was nothing either she or Ray could do to minimise that risk.

His fate was now in the hands of others.

***

At around the same time that Jan's train was pulling into Colchester Station, four men gathered around a meeting table in NCA headquarters. In addition to Wilpshire and Copeland — in whose office the meeting was taking place — there was Piers Wallace, head of the NCA's intelligence unit, and Jason Kennedy, the agency's head of cyber intelligence. Behind them, a laptop was linked to a projector aimed at a screen which had descended from the ceiling.

Once again, Copeland insisted on the proprieties, distributing coffee, tea or mineral water before business began. When all were settled, he launched into the briefing.

'Gentlemen, for the last two or three months we have had an agent undercover in an organisation which we believe is solely responsible for

137

the trafficking of young women into this country for the purposes of prostitution. This same organisation is also responsible for more general human trafficking as well as the importation and distribution of an industrial quantity of Class A drugs and of firearms and ammunition. It's also possible that it acts as middleman in deals to secure weapons for terrorist organisations around the world.

'In fact, this organisation has so many different branches, all operating individually and on a cellular basis, we have given it the codename Hydra, after the many-headed beast of Greek mythology. We know it has bought influence at the highest level throughout the British establishment but until now we have had no proof.

'What I am about to show you constitutes the best evidence we have about the extent of the Hydra's reach. Needless to say, nothing — and I mean nothing; not even a gnat's fart — of what you are about to see leaves this room. Is that fully understood?'

Wallace and Kennedy both nodded their agreement.

'Very well...'

Using a small remote control, Copeland switched on the projector and dimmed the lights. He pressed "Play," put down the control and sat back with his arms folded defensively across his chest, as if somehow the action might offer a degree of protection against the assault on his sensibilities that was about to commence.

The first frame, perfectly in focus but dimly lit, showed a balding, middle-aged man with a flabby body and a paunchy belly, lying naked on a round, red satin sheeted bed. A young girl, probably no more than 20 years old, with crimson and pink dyed hair and also naked, knelt between his legs holding his erect penis.

The second frame was exactly the same composition and was taken from the same angle. But this time the girl was performing oral sex on the man.

The third frame, again from the same angle, showed the girl straddling the man, who was penetrating her. A look of ecstasy was flooded across his face. The girl wore a look of contempt.

A stage whisper of 'Fucking hell,' escaped from Wallace's lips.

Copeland allowed the slide show to continue for another ten minutes and featuring another five men before he stopped it and switched the lights back on.

'What you have just seen gentlemen is the tip of the iceberg. We have in our possession 8,720 similar images. We believe that all the men in them hold positions of influence in our society. They are judges, lawyers, senior police officers, Members of Parliament, newspaper editors, eminent doctors, political figures, celebrities. But they have all succumbed to oldest lure of all: the siren song of female temptation.

'The task we face is in identifying as many of these men as we can, using as few resources as possible — as I've already impressed upon you, the fewer people who know about this, the better the chances of our success and the safer our man in the field will be.'

Wallace replied: 'I think it will be virtually impossible to identify a significant number of faces without outside help. I mean, unless it's someone really well known like a Cabinet minister or a pop star, the chances of us recognising them are pretty remote.'

'Piers, you can use whatever assistance you need,' Copeland said. 'I just don't want dozens of people getting a sniff of what we've got. If that happens, it's bound to leak.'

Turning to Kennedy, he placed two of the flash drives Jan had delivered on the table.

'On these are the e-mail addresses from two accounts used by a man we think is head of the Hydra. One is his regular business account but the other is a secret one he runs alongside it,' he said. 'Do what you need to do to get them hacked. And we also need taps on his mobile and landlines.'

'Not a problem,' Kennedy said. 'I can get that sorted.'

Copeland pursed his lips. 'I know you can. But remember the need for restraint in who we tell what. Whoever you pull in doesn't need to know about the photographs and vice-versa. Understand? My advice to you would be go to the very top. And even then be very, very careful. We don't know who's in those pictures yet.'

Copeland drained the cold dregs from his teacup. 'Right, thank you gentlemen. Let's reconvene here at ten o'clock Wednesday morning for an update.

After his three colleagues had left, Copeland went into the en-suite bathroom in his office, stripped off and stepped under a hot shower.

He felt grubby.

CHAPTER 18

Piers Wallace made sure his office door was firmly closed before he reached for his mobile phone. Even though the device used the encrypted voice protocol that was in every-day use by the intelligence services, law enforcement organisations and certain government departments, he did not want to run the risk of even his secretary overhearing his conversation.

He scrolled through his address book until he found the name he wanted and pressed the "call" button. It rang twice before a cultured voice answered: 'Piers, you old dog. Long time no speak to. I assume this is not a social call.'

'You never know Cammie, it could turn out that way. Still taking a splash with your malt?'

'I'd never drink it any other way,' replied Cameron McNeece. 'I drank it that way in the Mess for 25 years and I'll drink it that way until they put the lid on my box. Now, what can I do for you?'

McNeece had served in the Royal Air Force, retiring as head of photo-reconnaissance and interpretation with the rank of Group Captain and a reputation for being forthright, some might even say blunt. Now still only 58, he was as mentally agile and physically fit as men thirty years younger. He swam a mile every day except Sunday — when he cycled fifty miles instead — played squash twice a week and still found time to indulge his passion for golf.

'I've got some photographs I'd like you to take a look at, if you don't mind,' Wallace said.

'It would be my pleasure old man,' said McNeece. 'E-mail them over and tell me what you want from them.'

'I can't really do that.' He hesitated a second. 'There are over eight thousand of them.'

He imagined he heard McNeece choking into his mobile. 'Eight thousand? Christ, Piers, what the hell are they of?'

'I'd rather not say over the phone. Would you mind if I popped round with them?'

'I suppose you'd better if there's eight bloody thousand of them. Can you come straight away? I've got a meeting at four and I'm out all day tomorrow.'

'No problem Cammie. See you presently.'

***

It took the taxi less than ten minutes to reach Thames House, the impressive Portland stone building on the banks of the river whose name it carries, that is the headquarters of MI5, Britain's domestic security agency. Wallace paid the fare and double checked that the priceless flash drive was secure in his pocket before he got out of the cab.

Cameron McNeece had been a civilian for less than a week when he was recruited by MI5. The agency's Director General had worked with him several times and had been impressed by his uncanny knack of seeing things in photographs that others missed, a skill that had earned him the nickname "Hawkeye." As soon as he became aware that McNeece had taken off his uniform for the last time, he made a move to bring him on board. McNeece, who secretly detested the idea of quiet, untroubled days doing nothing, readily accepted.

As Wallace entered his office, McNeece greeted him like a long-lost brother, even though it had only been a few weeks since they had last met at a multi-agency conference in one of the large country mansions that the Government uses for such occasions.

'Good to see you old man. And I do believe it's your round,' he exclaimed.

'It will be my pleasure Cammie, once we get this little job out of the way. In fact, I might even run to dinner.'

'In that case, the sooner we get it cracked, the sooner we eat. What have you got for me?'

Wallace produced the flash drive from his pocket and put it down on McNeece's desk. 'This contains 8,720 photographs of men with young women in a variety of positions that would make a whorehouse madam blush. I need your help to identify them — the men that is; we're not worried about the women at this stage.'

Although the NCA had facial recognition software, he knew that MI5 had a much more powerful version. The software he had access to was very good at matching pin-sharp images with mug-shots from police files. But the version that MI5 had could make a match from images that had been taken on long lenses; that were a bit blurry or that didn't always show a full face.

He also knew that the agency kept a database of photographs of totally innocent but well-known people on the basis of "you never know when." It contained a host of candid shots of politicians, journalists, lawyers, doctors, authors, media personalities and celebrities, including some of the more obscure ones and activists of every hue. In fact, just about everyone who had a public face.

It was one of those security assets that was never publicly admitted to, nor ever discussed outside a tight circle. Wallace was only aware of its existence because McNeece had alluded to it after one too many malt whiskies at a country house conference.

McNeece picked up the flash drive and turned it over and over through his fingers.

'Can I ask why?' he ventured. 'Why do you need to know who these men are?'

'I can't tell you that right now Cammie,' Wallace replied. 'But believe me, it is very, very important. And I know you have — what shall we say? — special facilities that I don't have that will help you do it.'

McNeece eyed Wallace deeply for several seconds, trying to puzzle out how the NCA man knew of the secret database, having forgotten his drink-induced indiscretion.

Eventually he said: 'Alright Piers, I'll do it for you. But be aware it will take a while, possibly as long as a month. And when I claim that dinner, I might also fine you a bottle of '96 Pauillac.'

'If you can pull this off, it will be my pleasure,' Wallace said.

***

Jason Kennedy had taken Bernard Copeland's advice when it came to obtaining authorisation to hack Mike Pilling's e-mail accounts and tap his telephones. But the Attorney General was proving problematic. He couldn't see why someone he thought of as merely a computer nerd, albeit the top computer nerd in the National Crime Agency, should be granted an audience.

After several days of trying, though, Kennedy's persistence — and an abundant amount of name dropping — paid dividends and he was allotted 15 minutes of the AG's time and not one second more.

Rupert Pitt-Russell QC, MP, was the country's top lawyer, responsible for giving legal advice to the Government and the Crown. A serving Member of Parliament for the past 15 years, he also fitted the Dickensian perception of a politician. Even though he was still in his 40s, his ample stomach, over which was stretched a dark three-piece suit, complete with silver watch chain, his prematurely grey hair and similarly coloured lamb-chop sideburns, combined to make him look much older. This image was not helped by his habit of wearing half-moon reading glasses, over which he peered at everyone who sat before him. Naturally, he had a sceptical attitude towards electronic gadgets and those who claimed to understand them.

'Yes. What do you want?' he barked at Kennedy, waving his hand at a chair in an uncertain invitation for him to sit.

'Well sir, I'm from the National Crime Agency...'

'Yes, yes, I know that. What do you want?'

'I need your authorisation to begin surveillance on several e-mail addresses and telephone lines,' said Kennedy nervously.

'And why, exactly, have you come to me for that consent and not a judge in chambers?'

Kennedy coughed to clear his throat. 'Well sir, it's a very delicate matter. We are currently investigating a criminal organisation that we believe has bought itself influence at the highest levels, including in the judiciary itself.'

He stopped speaking.

'Go on. Go on' demanded Pitt-Russell impatiently.

'The thing is, we don't know exactly who's involved and we can't take the risk of a leak. We have a man undercover whose life could be at risk. That's why I was told to go to the very top,' Kennedy explained. 'That's why I've come to you.'

'And whose e-mails and telephones do you intend to tap?'

'They belong to the man we believe is the head of the organisation. We're trying to identify who he may have in his pocket and these intercepts would help that process greatly.'

Pitt-Russell slumped backwards into his high-backed green leather chair, upon which the Crown coat of arms was embossed in gold. He folded chubby fingers over his stomach and began to flick the watch chain with his thumbs. Unblinking, he scrutinised Kennedy over his half-moon spectacles, as if searching for some flaw that might give him grounds to refuse the request.

'How long do you need?' he eventually asked.

'That's not an easy question to answer sir,' said Kennedy. 'It's an on-going operation. It could take months before we get a result.'

'I'll give you three months. If you need more, you'll have to come back to me. Understood?'

'Yes sir. Perfectly sir.'

'Are you in Old Queen Street?'

'Yes sir.'

'Right, I'll get the necessary paper work biked over to you but you can go ahead and begin your intercepts.'

'Thank you sir. And thank you for your time,' Kennedy said, rising from the chair and making for the door.

Before he got there, Pitt-Russell spoke again. This time his tone was softer.

'One more thing... good luck. I hate bent lawyers but I hate bent judges more.'

***

To the people who work there it is known as "The Doughnut'; the circular, futuristically designed building that houses GCHQ, an acronym that stands for Government Communications Headquarters. It is the third arm of Britain's security network and works hand-in-glove with MI5 and MI6, the Secret Intelligence Service, to protect the country from threats posed by foreign governments, terrorist organisations, cyber criminals or anyone else who nurses a desire to do damage to the nation.

Built in the suburbs of the genteel town of Cheltenham, The Doughnut is so vast, the Albert Hall, London's world-class concert venue, would fit inside its central courtyard. Its history goes back to the First World War and the development of "Sigint" — signals intelligence — at the hands of the emerging Government Code and Cypher School, the unit that went on to form the basis of the team at Bletchley Park which would crack the German Enigma Codes during the Second World War.

Today, GCHQ employs an army of mathematicians, linguists, cryptographers and analysts in any number of specialities. So when the order came down to tap the telephone numbers and hack into the e-mail addresses associated with the Hydra, no one batted an eyelid. It was just another job to do.

Among the many tools at the disposal of GCHQ staff is a piece of software that has the ability to sift vast amounts of data, mine it, discover hidden nuggets of information and then identify underlying themes and trends.

It was a tool that was to prove invaluable in the battle against the Hydra.

CHAPTER 19

Ray was on the road again, this time heading north for the container terminal at the port of Immingham on the southern shores of the River Humber. And he was not happy. He was not happy because sitting alongside him in the 40-tonne truck's cab was George Curtis, the living barrel who was Pilling's right-hand man and who, Ray knew, was just waiting for an excuse to inflict a great deal of damage on him.

But the real reason for his disquiet was the fact that he was driving an unbranded tractor unit pulling an empty container trailer, both of which were carrying false number plates, to collect an unknown cargo for an unknown destination. What he did not know was that any policeman who bothered to check the plates would find that they related to an identical white lorry that was registered to a transport company called Conti-Trans with an address on an industrial estate on the outskirts of Swansea.

And if that same policeman bothered to ring the company he would be connected to an answering machine on which the voice of Summer Long would deliver the message: 'You have reached the offices of Conti-Trans international transport. Sorry but the offices are currently closed. Please leave your name, number and a brief message and we will get back to you as soon as possible.' Even though it was a Swansea telephone number, the answering machine sat in a locked cupboard next to Summer's desk 260 miles away in Colchester.

Ray had been told only that he had to collect a specific container at a specific time in Immingham. He hadn't been told what was in it or where it had to be taken but he could hazard a very good guess, a guess he considered confirmed by the presence of Curtis.

The 163-mile journey took them along a series of A roads, across Norfolk, skirting The Wash, and on into Lincolnshire. Apart from working for the same master, Ray and Curtis had nothing in common. Despite that, he had tried to make the trip lighter by making small talk. Curtis, however, was wearing his uncommunicative head and answered only in a string of grunts. To lighten the atmosphere he turned on the radio but Curtis turned it off again without a word.

Eventually, Curtis's closely-cropped head of blonde hair began to droop. Then it lolled against the side window and he began to snore. Unseen by Ray, saliva dribbled from the left side of his mouth. At least it meant he could concentrate on driving without the palpable tension of silence between them.

A shade over four hours after leaving Colchester, Ray was at Immingham Docks and had found his way to the container terminal. What he saw there forced him to a stop dead.

'George, George,' he said insistently to the still-slumbering bulk. 'Wake up. We've got a problem.'

After a few grunts and snorts and half-muttered oaths, Curtis was staring out through the windscreen at the scene that had pulled Ray up short but had, at the same time, validated his suspicions.

The road ahead was blocked by two police cars. Beyond them, both men could see more police vehicles and three ambulances. There was a lot of frenzied activity but no clear sign of what the problem actually was. One of the police officers manning the roadblock walked towards them.

'Sorry lads,' he said as Ray opened his window. 'The container terminal's closed for now.'

'What's the problem officer?' Ray asked. 'We've got to pick up a container from Denmark.'

'There's been an incident. It'll be a few hours yet before you can get in.'

'What's happened?'

'We've found some illegals in a container. Can't tell you anything more,' the constable replied. 'Where are you lads from anyway?'

Ray realised they were on the verge of arousing suspicions and was deliberately vague in his response.

'We've come over from Merseyside. But we'll find somewhere to park up and come back later. Can I turn round up there?'

'Yeah. There's a mini-roundabout up there where you should be able to manage.'

As he executed the turn to take them back out of the dock, Ray noticed that the colour had drained from Curtis's moon face and he was trying to key a number into his mobile with trembling fingers.

'Mike, we've got a big problem,' he began when his call was answered. 'Looks like Plod found our cargo before we could get to it. There's cops and ambulances all over the place. The terminal's closed.'

Ray couldn't hear Pilling's response but didn't need any sound to know what it would be.

'No, no. We're alright,' Curtis went on. 'Welbourne did a good job of giving them a bum steer when they got nosy. Told them we'd come from Liverpool to collect a container from Denmark.'

The conversation over, Curtis ordered: 'Right. Get us the fuck out of here.'

Feigning naivety, Ray asked; 'What about the cargo?'

'It's too fucking late for them. Just head for home.'

They had been on the road for only fifteen minutes or so when BBC Radio 5 Live broadcast the first indications of what had happened at Immingham.

'*Reports are coming in that a woman and a child have been found dead inside a shipping container at Immingham Docks on the Humber,*' the presenter reported. '*A number of other people also found in the container have been taken to hospital for treatment.*'

As their journey continued, more and more information was broadcast.

First: *It was believed there were up to 20 people in the container, which was on a lorry that been loaded onto a ship in Cuxhaven, Germany. One of the people was seriously ill after suffering a heart attack. The others were being treated for dehydration and hypothermia.*

Later: *The two people who died were thought to be a mother and her eight year-old son. It was not known where, or how, they had got into the container. Police in Immingham had detained a 35 year-old German lorry driver for questioning.*

A bulletin two hours later: *Police had established that there were eighteen people in the container, including the two who had died. All had come from Somalia in East Africa and were thought to have been in the container for up to 24 hours. Detectives and Border Force officers were waiting to interview the survivors to establish how and when they had travelled from their homelands to Germany.*

And as the artic entered the outskirts of Colchester: *Police were searching for the driver from a Swansea-based haulage company that was scheduled to collect the container from Immingham. There were no records of him having arrived at the port.*

'Looks like your bullshit did the job Welbourne,' said Curtis, putting both feet onto the lorry's dashboard. 'Well done.'

'We might not be out of the woods yet,' Ray cautioned. 'I don't know how Swansea has come into this but it won't take 'em long to realise they're barking up the wrong tree.'

Curtis smirked and said: 'Yeah, but as long as they don't come pissing on our tree we'll be alright.'

When they finally arrived at the Pilling Transport depot, Mike Pilling was his usual charming self. He looked up from his position leaning over Summer's left shoulder, a position that gave the Ray the distinct impression he had been staring down her blouse. He eyed the two men carefully, as if mentally counting that they had all their limbs intact.

'Right George. In here, now,' he rasped, jerking a thumb towards his office.

The door closed with a bang.

'Oops,' said Summer.

Inside the office, Curtis could see that Pilling's anxiety levels were rising rapidly and set about trying to reduce them.

'Welbourne did well feeding them all that crap,' he said. 'According to the radio, the cops are after some geezer from a transport company in Swansea. And they've nicked the German who was driving the lorry so it looks like we're in the clear.'

Pilling's face went puce. 'You fucking idiot George,' he shouted. 'Don't you realise that German is one of ours? He knows exactly how those people got into that container — he fucking put them there. He knows how they got to Germany. He knows fucking everything. If he talks it's good fucking night Vienna for all of us.'

'Oh shit Mike. What are we going to do?'

'What am *I* going to do George? What am *I* going to do? There's no "we" in this. There's only one thing I can do. I'm going to have to talk to Frank Chiswell.'

'Chiswell? That psycho who gutted the girl and left her tied to Southend pier?' Even Curtis was astounded. 'Christ Mike, that's a bit desperation stakes.'

'Desperate times my friend; desperate times.'

The two detectives had already driven round the industrial estate twice but could find no sign of Conti-Trans international transport. Indeed, they could find no sign of anything that looked even remotely like a transport company, international or otherwise. They had called back to the station to double-check the address and were on the verge of giving up.

'Stop. That's it. It's there,' yelled Hywel Tudor from the passenger seat.

Behind the wheel, Iaon Griffiths stood on the brakes instinctively. 'Where?'

'There. On the right. That's it. Unit Seventeen.'

Griffiths looked uncertainly at the building his colleague was pointing at. It was Unit Seventeen right enough. But across the front, the company title declared itself: "Party On Down" and underneath: "All your party supplies. Wholesale and Retail."

The two men got out of their car and walked up to the building, a single storey in a row of identical properties, each with an office frontage and a roller-shuttered loading bay alongside. The door was locked but the buzz of an automatic lock signalled that their presence had been noted.

Inside, a well-built woman of about 40 in a black sleeveless dress got up from a desk and waddled towards the service counter. The top of her right arm displayed a full colour tattoo of a tiger's head with a cobra in its mouth. Around her left bicep was a Maori-style pattern and the inside of each wrist was decorated with single words which could have been from any language in the world.

'Yes lads. What can I do for you?' she asked.

Probably not much, Tudor thought unkindly. 'We're looking for Conti-Trans international transport,' he said. 'Ever heard of it?'

A puzzled expression crossed the woman's face. 'Conti-Trans? No, can't say I have,' she said. 'What's the address?'

'Here. Unit Seventeen,' said Griffiths. 'It's obvious you're not it but any ideas?'

The woman turned to the open-plan office, where half a dozen or so other women were keeping their heads down. 'Anybody heard of Conti-Trans transport?' she yelled. 'Supposed to be here at this address.'

The question was answered with several head shakes, a couple of 'Never heard of it' and a definitive 'It's not on this estate.'

'Are there are any transport companies on this estate?' Griffiths asked and was met once again with a wall of negative responses.

'Oh well. Thanks for your time ladies,' Tudor said, closing the door behind them.

By the end of the following day, the two policemen had had identical reactions at every industrial estate within 10 miles of Swansea city centre. When they reported the fact to their colleagues in Lincolnshire, the news was met with a degree of disbelief.

'But that's the name and address Immingham Docks has for the transport company that was meant to collect the container,' a detective sergeant who had answered the phone protested.

'Yeah, well, our inquiries show there's no such company; not in South Wales at least,' Tudor said. 'Do you have a phone number?'

'We have the one that was given to the shipping company. It's a Swansea dialling code but it goes straight to an answering machine,' said the sergeant. 'We've left a message but there's been no call back and, to be honest, I don't expect one.' Tudor suggested: 'What about the driver? Does he know anything about Conti-Trans?'

'He says not. But then again he knows the square root of fuck all. We've let him go.'

***

The story only made a few paragraphs in four of Britain's national newspapers, for even though it was just a week after the discovery of two dead bodies and 16 illegal immigrants in a container at Immingham Docks, other stories were now occupying the headlines. Even the newspapers that published it hadn't bothered to pursue their own inquiries, instead taking the copy filed by one of the pan-European news agencies at its face value.

It said that the man police had questioned over the tragic deaths at Immingham Docks had been found dead in the River Elbe at Cuxhaven. He was believed to have drowned. A couple more paragraphs recounted the discovery of the Somalis.

When the German police announced the discovery of the truck driver's body and the fact that he was believed to have drowned, they were acting somewhat prematurely, because they had not received the post-mortem examination report. It would reveal that the 35 year-old had indeed drowned. But the water in his lungs was fresh water. From a tap. Not the mixture of salt and fresh water, diesel and other substances that could generally be expected to be found in a busy industrialised river like the Elbe.

The examination would also reveal the body had what appeared to be rope burns around its wrists and ankles and bruising to the throat and windpipe. The pathologist concluded the unfortunate man had been tied down and held by the neck while his mouth and nose were constantly filled with fresh water until he couldn't breathe any longer and drowned. He was already dead when he was dumped in the river.

***

On the day after the discovery of the Somalis in Immingham, the GCHQ tap on Mike Pilling's mobile recorded a call to a pay-as-you-go mobile in Bonn. A voice later identified as Pilling's had said: 'We need to look after our friend the delivery driver. Do you know him?'

Voice recognition software had potentially identified the call recipient as Frank Chiswell, who was wanted in connection with the death of an 18 year-old Romanian girl in Southend. He had replied: 'Yeah. Leave it to me.'

Thirty six hours later, Pilling had received an incoming call from the German mobile in which the caller had simply said: 'It's done.'

Nothing more was said by either man but the sophisticated software used by GCHQ made a connection between the location of the pay-as-you-go mobile, the phrase "delivery driver" and the death of the German trucker in Cuxhaven. The link was noted by one of the organisation's serious crime analysts and stored for further development.

CHAPTER 20

Two weeks passed before there was another significant development that triggered any interest in Cheltenham. The watchers assigned to monitor Mike Pilling's e-mail and mobile phone traffic were alerted to a call he received from a satellite telephone. Data gathered from four communications satellites in geo-stationary orbit identified the location of the call as a remote spot in the hills surrounding the beautiful village of Raggiolo in Tuscany, Italy.

Images from a spy satellite further pinpointed the call to a luxurious villa set amongst woodland. If the technician operating the satellite had zoomed in on the target, he would have seen a large, modern home set into the hillside and — apart from the heavy, imposing wooden gates that protected it — totally invisible from the single-track road which ran past it.

He might have lingered over the cluster of cars parked in the front courtyard around an elaborate marble fountain, a collection which included a Bugatti Veyron, one of the world's most expensive cars, a Range Rover and a Bentley Continental. Further investigation would have revealed the back of the villa was two floors lower than the front and featured expansive windows to take advantage of the stunning vista of the valley that opened up to the south, bathing the house in sunlight from dawn to dusk.

And if he had been really nosy, he would have seen a young woman reclining on a sun lounger by the pool. She was naked apart from a tiny bikini bottom that consisted of nothing more than a miniscule triangle of silk, held in place by what appeared to be a piece of ribbon and which gave a mere passing nod to modesty. Waist length auburn hair tumbled over her breasts. A pair of tortoise shell Gucci sunglasses shielded her deep green eyes from the glare. By her side lay two Neopolitan Mastiffs and an ice bucket containing a bottle of Cristal champagne, which she was drinking from an antique lead-crystal glass.

Adelina Dalla Montagna had never wanted for anything. At least, not since the evening 12 years before when a handsome Turkish man had walked into the lap-dancing club in Milan where her perfect lithe figure and olive skin had made her a favourite attraction amongst the customers. He did not want to pay 25 Euro for a dance. He did not want to pay 50 Euro for a fully nude dance. He wanted her. He offered her 5,000 Euro to spend the night with him. She accepted and never returned to her former life.

He installed her in the villa above Raggiolo and lavished upon her whatever her heart desired. It was he who had changed her name from Elisabetta Barsotti, the name that had she had found perfectly acceptable for the previous 18 years of her life, telling her that Adelina was an Italian form of a Latin name that meant "Little Noble." She knew that Dalla Montagna meant "From the mountains."

Her new persona, she believed, summed up everything she sought to be and she tried her level best to live up to her own expectations every moment of the day.

She lived like a princess in isolated splendour with a maid and chauffeur, who also doubled as a bodyguard, to look after her. Kamil Behar, her Turkish lover, spent long periods of time away from her on business but when he returned they spent hour after hour simply enjoying each others' bodies, drinking the finest French champagne and gorging themselves on the delicious food prepared and served by the maid.

Adelina had no way of knowing that Behar had another lover who lived in much more modest circumstances in the city of Leeds in England but for whom he paid the rent and all her bills in exchange for nights of unbounded passion whenever he visited the UK.

And she thought it politic not to mention to Behar that the chauffeur-cum-bodyguard he had hired was also an energetic lover when he wasn't busy servicing the maid. Or that when winter descended upon the hills and snow blocked the road, the three of them occasionally kept each other warm with steamy sex sessions in front of the roaring fire.

Then one day a lawyer from Milan appeared at the door. He told her that Behar had been shot dead by British police in circumstances that were not exactly clear to him. All he knew was that the incident was reported to have included hostages, one of whom was a British police officer who was apparently known to Behar. His name was Raymond Wilson.

Her grief was instantaneous, intense and loudly expressed but was somewhat eased by the next piece of news the lawyer gave her. Behar

154

had left everything he owned in the world to her, including his business interests.

Those business interests included the organisation to which Britain's National Crime Agency had assigned the codename Hydra. She rapidly absorbed how the organisation made its money; how its individual strands worked, separately and together, to ensure she could continue to live the life to which she had become accustomed.

She therefore put considerable effort into making sure that the money-making machine continued to work perfectly and to her benefit. She enforced her will on the people who ran Hydra with a viciousness and violence that would have made Behar proud. On her orders men — and occasionally women — had been maimed, mutilated and murdered, sometimes for seemingly minor transgressions. But whenever she was displeased, someone paid the price.

It was the bodyguard, Gennaro, who drew her attention to the incident at Immingham Docks in which a mother and son had died in a locked container and to the subsequent discovery of the body of a trucker who had been interviewed by police in connection with the deaths.

She had called Mike Pilling at once and even though she did not put down her glass of Cristal — refilled by Gennaro without bidding — she dismissed his initial attempts at small talk with barely disguised contempt, just to emphasise her importance.

'Michael I am reading things in the newspapers that disturb me. What the fuck is going on?' she demanded.

'Don't worry Adelina, everything's under control,' he replied calmly.

'There is no connection?'

'Not now. The only connection has been, er, cut.'

'So you can assure me there is no interruption to trade?'

'No there isn't. But you are aware of the loss of one of the means of transport aren't you?'

'Loss? What do mean loss?' The anger was beginning to rise in her voice.

'It was seized by the authorities. In the North Sea. There were twelve women on board; women I had ear-marked for...'

'Jesus Christ Pilling. Can I not trust you with anything? I'm coming to see you.'

She abruptly ended the call, drained the glass of champagne and said to Gennaro: 'Ring the airport and tell them to get the jet ready. I'm going to England tomorrow morning. Then ring London and tell them I will be using the flat.' She stroked the inside of his thigh and added: 'And you're coming with me.'

At GCHQ, the software that had identified the sat-phone call's recipient as Pilling made a contextual link between what had been said during the call, the Immingham deaths and the recovery of the body in Cuxhaven. Coupled with the knowledge that Adelina Dalla Montagne was planning to visit Britain, the crime analyst decided it was time to ring Bernard Copeland at the NCA.

Just after lunchtime the following day, a snow-white Gulfstream G550 executive jet landed at Biggin Hill Airport in Kent. Even though the day was overcast and dull, Adelina wore her Gucci sunglasses as she and Gennaro were escorted into the executive terminal where immigration officers gave their passports only a cursory glance before wishing them both a pleasant stay in the city.

Minutes later, they were in the back of a Bentley limousine heading for Adelina's London "flat" which was actually a luxurious apartment on the 10th floor of one of the city's most prestigious addresses.

But long before they arrived the NCA knew they were in the country.

***

Across the city, the telephone rang on Piers Wallace's desk at NCA headquarters.

'Piers, it's Cammie,' a voice said. 'I've got that information you asked me for.'

Cammie was Cameron McNeece, MI5's photo-intelligence officer, who Wallace had asked to help identify the men photographed with young women that Ray had found in Mike Pilling's hidden studio.

'Thanks Cammie. I'm on my way,' replied Wallace, dropping the phone back into its cradle as he stood to head for the door.

McNeece, never a man to mince words, got straight down to business. Pleasantries could come later.

'Right Piers, I won't pretend this has been easy because it hasn't but I have got you a result which I think you will find acceptable,' he began. 'From the 8,720 images, we have managed to identify 621 individuals, each of whom features in an average of 10 shots each. Using the same average, that leaves some 251 individuals for whom, as yet, we have no positive identification but we're still working on it.

'Of the 621 men we have identified, one is a serving member of the Cabinet and five others have served as ministers either in the present Administration or previous ones. There are 37 serving Members of Parliament, eight highly placed civil servants and 40 lower ranked ones.

'Incidentally, one of the senior civil servants held high office in the Crown Prosecution Service but his body was fished out of the Thames a few weeks ago, so you've no need to worry about him.

'There are five High Court judges, 29 barristers and 52 solicitors, the majority of whom practise criminal law but a clutch of them have specialities such as tax law and, surprisingly, divorce. Two of the men in the pictures are current editors of national newspapers and five others are specialist correspondents for them. There are two trade union general secretaries, one of whom is known to hold extreme left-wing views and three others who hold executive positions in well-known and popular charities. The rest are a mix of actors, television presenters, sportsmen and what I suppose one would refer to as minor celebrities.

'It's quite a mix. There's the full list.' He flicked a brown A4 envelope across his desk. 'I don't suppose you are going to tell me why they're important, so the only question I can ask is when can I claim my 96 Pauillac?'

Wallace picked up the envelope and ran it through his fingers, as if by touching it, he could absorb its explosive contents. 'Cammie, I am eternally grateful to you for this and I think you're entitled to know why these pictures are so important to us. We're currently investigating a major crime organisation that appears to have bought itself influence in some very high places. We believe the men in these pictures have all been trapped in the organisation's web. These images are the whip hand that is being held over them. I'm sure you can now see why their identities are so important to us. So, when are you available to claim your 96 Pauillac and, more importantly, where do you want to take it? Along with the lumpy bits it will accompany, that is.'

***

Adelina stepped from the shower and wrapped herself in a huge, thick, fluffy white towel. She bundled her long hair into a smaller one and walked back into the bedroom where Gennaro was now asleep, exhausted by her vigorous sexual demands.

As she did so, her sat-phone rang. It was the very latest technology, vastly different from the clunky sat-phones of old with their awkward aerial that had to be pointed at a precise angle to get a signal. This one was a sleeve into which an ordinary mobile phone was clipped, connected via Bluetooth. Apart from the stumpy aerial, it was difficult to distinguish it from an everyday mobile.

The voice at the other end did not identify himself or check that he was speaking to the right person. He said simply: 'You have been infiltrated.'

'What?'

'The National Crime Agency has got a man undercover inside your organisation.'

Before Adelina could ask any questions, the caller hung up, leaving her staring in disbelief at the handset.

'Gennaro, Gennaro, wake up. We have to go to Colchester. Now.'

The watchers at GCHQ had heard the conversation too. Its importance was not lost on them, but what caused them more concern was the origin of the call.

It had come from a mobile on the Government secure network.

Bernard Copeland felt the blood drain from his face when he received the news. Ray Wilson was compromised. Hydra knew they had been infiltrated and it wouldn't take them long to work out that Ray was the spy in the camp. He had to be extracted at once. His life was on the line.

Less than a mile away, a chauffeur-driven Bentley purred from a car park below a block of luxury apartments as the driver keyed a destination into the sat-nav. Colchester.

CHAPTER 21

Summer stared open-mouthed at the elegant woman who stepped from the back of the chauffeur-driven limousine that had just pulled up outside her office window. She was hypnotised by the beautiful cut of the woman's clothes; by the way her hair cascaded over her shoulders; by the way she appeared to glide over the ground. She was the kind of woman Summer had only ever seen in magazines — and she was heading straight for her door.

When the door opened, Summer was amazed to see a man standing there; her first impression had been that the woman was alone. Like the woman he was immaculately dressed; in his case in an expensive dark suit with a crisp, white open-necked shirt. He said nothing but stood back to hold the door open for the elegant woman, who paused and glanced around the office as if discomfited by the spartan surroundings.

'I want Michael Pilling,' she said softly in perfect English that carried only a trace of her native Italian.

'I'll, er, I'll see if he's available,' Summer replied nervously. 'Who shall I say wants him?'

'He will be available,' the woman said, more harshly. 'Tell him it is Adelina. He will know who I am.'

She had barely finished speaking when Pilling appeared from his office. He too had watched the Bentley pull into his yard and stop in front of the office. He too had watched the chic beauty climb out. And now he knew who she was.

'Adelina, Mike Pilling,' he said, holding out his hand as he advanced towards the counter flap. 'Do come in.'

Adelina deliberately ignored the offered hand but, with Gennaro close enough to be a shadow, moved towards Pilling's inner sanctum.

'Summer, will you organise coffee for our guests please?' Pilling asked his still-stunned secretary.

Adelina stopped. 'Is it proper coffee?' she asked.

'Er, sorry, er, no. It's instant,' Summer replied.

'In that case not for me. I don't drink that rubbish,' Adelina said.

'Perhaps some sparkling mineral water then,' suggested Pilling, ushering the Italians into his office. As he did so he mouthed to Summer: 'Go and buy some, quick.'

Inside the office, Adelina and Gennaro were already sitting side by side on the sofa. Although he knew who they were, it was the first time Pilling had seen either of them and like so many men in her life, he was mesmerised by Adelina's beauty.

'I hope you had a pleasant journey,' he ventured as an ice-breaker.

'We're not here to make small talk Michael,' she rebuked. 'We have a very serious problem that needs to be rectified urgently.'

'Problem?'

'Yes. We have a spy in the camp. Your National Crime Agency has someone working undercover in the organisation. It has to be here in the UK.'

She let the statement hang, at the same time studying Pilling's face to gauge his reaction to the devastating news. What she saw was genuine shock underpinned by a clarity of thought.

'Welbourne. It has to be Welbourne,' he said.

'Who is Welbourne?' Adelina asked.

'My last recruit. He came here looking for a job a few months ago. He seemed ideal — ex-British Army, could drive a truck and handle himself, knew his way around firearms and wasn't afraid to get his hands dirty. I tried him out on a few low-level jobs and he didn't let me down so I let him loose on a few bigger ones. He got himself into a few tight corners but managed to get himself out of them so I trusted him more and more. It can only be him.'

Adelina scrutinised Pilling carefully. 'How can you be so sure? It's a very big organisation.'

'Yes, but the hub of it is here in this depot. And everyone who works here has worked here for years. I know them all personally and trust every single one of them. Welbourne's the new-comer. He's the one I know least about. It all fits.'

'So where is he now?'

Pilling stood, walked to his office door and asked Summer: 'Where's Ray Welbourne right now?'

'He's taking a load of used car parts from Birmingham to Felixstowe. He's due back in a couple of hours.'

Adelina pricked up her ears when she heard the name Ray. There were thousands of British men called Ray. It had to be a coincidence. But then, Pilling suspected this man was the infiltrator, the spy in the camp. Could it be that her greatest wish in the world was about to come true? Surely it was too much to hope.

When Pilling turned back into the room she said: 'You know, I've been told that my Kamil was shot dead by British police in an incident that involved a policeman called Ray Wilson. I am sure it's nothing more than mere coincidence that the man you think is the NCA's undercover man is called Ray. But I would be very, very pleased if it did turn out to be the same man.'

'Well, when he gets here, you can ask him yourself,' Pilling replied with an evil grin.

Still framed in the doorway, Pilling spoke to Summer once more. 'Find George Curtis and tell him I need him here immediately. Then go home and take some time off. I'll ring you when I need you back.'

'But Mike...' she began.

'Don't argue Summer. Just do as you're told.'

He returned to his desk, sat down heavily and threw his feet onto the steel desk's rubber topping.

'Now all we have to do is wait,' he announced.

***

For the previous eight hours, ever since she had taken the phone call from Bernard Copeland that had set her heart racing, Jan Holroyd had been desperately trying to contact Ray. Her phone calls had gone to voicemail and her increasingly frantic messages had gone unanswered. Likewise, her text messages were unacknowledged. She had banged on the door of his flat to no avail and even pushed a note through the letterbox.

But still there had been no word from Ray.

He had stumbled out of bed shortly before 5.am, managed a quick shave and a cup of tea before heading for the depot and the start of that day's run to Birmingham and Felixstowe. He had been on the road for an hour before he realised that his mobile phone was still on the cabinet at the side of his bed. He was uncontactable and reliant on public telephones if he needed to speak to someone.

It felt strangely liberating. But with the feeling of liberation came another, more ominous, feeling. Of vulnerability.

The sun had already begun to slip behind the Colchester skyline when Ray arrived back at the depot. Pilling's white Mercedes was parked in its usual spot but everywhere else was deserted, the workshop long closed, the office in darkness, all the staff either at home with their families or enjoying an early evening beer. He manoeuvred the lorry and its now-empty trailer into a parking bay, switched off the ignition and sat for a moment while he gathered his thoughts. He would call Jan, see if she fancied a beer. He needed to catch up with her because he needed to know what was happening with the information he had provided. But first of all a long, hot shower was in order.

He climbed down from the cab and was just about to lock the door when his world went black. Something had been thrust over his head and was being pulled tight around his neck.

Ray's first instinct was to try to pull the hood away from his throat so he could breathe; he kicked out blindly to no effect and tried to shout. Then he crumpled in pain as something hard and heavy hit him behind his knees. At the same time his brain registered a vivid flash of red, orange and white and a blinding pain as he was clubbed across his left temple.

He had no concept of how long he had been out when a bucket of cold water, rapidly followed by another, shocked him back to consciousness. He was aware of being shackled hand and foot, in an X-cruciform shape, to the corners of some kind of metal frame. He could feel the chill of heavy wire against his back and realised he was naked apart from his boxer shorts. There were other people in the room but they were masked from him by the hood that remained in place over his head.

'Get that fucking hood off him. Let's take a look at the bastard,' said a voice he recognised as Pilling's.

The hood was violently snatched from his head and Ray found himself staring at the grinning face of George Curtis, who grunted: 'Fuck pig,' before spitting in his eyes.

As the spittle dribbled away and he became more used to the gloom, Ray recognised that he was in one of the disused offices in what he had come to know as "Mike's Shed."

Next second his head was spinning, full of flashing lights once more as Curtis drove hard punches to his face and body.

'Steady on George. We need him to talk,' an unseen Pilling said.

'I just want to kill the twat,' Curtis responded.

'Yes, I know you do,' said Pilling. 'But we need information from him before you do. So let's be a little more, er, persuasive, shall we?'

'Alright boss. What do you want me to do to him?'

'Nothing for now. I think we'll leave him to stew for a bit. We'll come back later. See if he feels like co-operating.'

Curtis jammed the hood back over Ray's head and he heard people — more than the two he thought had been in the room — leaving.

***

By now Jan was becoming frantic. She had been unable to raise Ray on his mobile. He didn't appear to be in his flat and his car was nowhere to be seen at Pilling's depot — she had driven up there but all she saw was the white Mercedes parked outside what she knew to be the office block. Her mentors at the NCA could offer no advice other than 'Keep trying.'

She had to get inside his flat to see what clues there may be to his whereabouts, but she didn't have a key. There was only one thing to do. She dialled 999 and told the police she was worried about her boyfriend. She spun the call handler a line saying he had been depressed; she had tried umpteen times to call him on his mobile but every time it went to voicemail; she had been to his flat but couldn't get a reply; he was not at work and she was terrified he might have done something stupid.

It was a quiet night in Colchester so the call handler issued a "Concern for welfare" message, a call which was answered by PCs Robert Peters and Yvonne Houlihan. Within twenty minutes they were at Ray's address, where they found a genuinely anxious Jan pacing the pavement. She repeated everything she had told the call handler.

'Have you two had a row or anything?' asked Houlihan.

'No, not at all,' Jan replied. 'It's just that, well, I haven't spoken to him for a couple of days now and that's not normal. Even when he's away he always rings me at least once a day.'

Roberts, squarely built with a hint of curly black hair showing beneath his cap, stood with his hands resting inside his stab vest. 'Could he be with someone else? You know, another woman?'

'No, absolutely not. I trust him implicitly. I just know he's come to some harm.'

'OK then. Show us which flat it is.'

'That one there. To the right of the main entrance.'

To the surprise of all three, the main door swung open to the touch, unlocked despite being supposedly secured by an entry code system.

Roberts knocked on the door then squatted down, opened the letter box and took a deep sniff.

Jan was well aware of what he was smelling for but played dumb. 'What's he doing that for?' she asked Houlihan.

'Just checking to see if there's a gas leak or anything,' she replied.

He rattled the door, which gave a fraction of an inch.

'It's not very secure. It won't take much to open it,' he said to Jan. 'That is, if it's alright with you.'

'Yes, yes. Anything. Please.'

'OK, wait here. We've got the Big Key in the van.'

The Big Key was a 32lb steel battering ram, officially known as The Enforcer, specifically designed to open locked doors with the minimum of effort that was normally used on early morning raids. Within seconds of Roberts returning, casually swinging it from his right hand, the two police officers were standing inside Ray's flat.

Nothing was out of place. There was no washing up waiting to be done; no dirty cups dumped on the floor; the cushions on the sofa were neatly plumped; not a speck of dust anywhere. In the bedroom, the double bed showed signs of being slept in and the washing basket was half full. Apart from those few signs of habitation, it could have been a show flat.

'Does anything here look out of place Miss Holroyd,' asked Houlihan.

'No. The last time I was here was about a week ago and it looked exactly the same then,' Jan lied.

She wandered through to the bedroom and straight away spotted Ray's mobile on his bedside cabinet. A feeling of cold fear gripped her. Now she knew why he wasn't acknowledging her calls. He couldn't.

Wherever he was, whatever he was doing, he was on his own.

She slipped the device into her handbag to examine later. She turned and was startled to find that Houlihan was standing right behind her — but quickly realised the policewoman had not seen her take the phone.

'Well, Miss Holroyd, your boyfriend obviously isn't here,' she said. 'But if you're still concerned we can circulate his description, just in case any of our colleagues come across him. And we'll get someone round to fix that door in the morning.'

'Thank you, that's very kind. Thank you for what you've done, I'm really grateful.'

The police van had not even reached the end of the street before Jan was calling Bernard Copeland at home. Despite the lateness of the hour, he was neither cross nor surprised at the call.

'I just know he's in trouble sir,' she said. 'I found his mobile in his flat, that's why he's not been responding but there's no sign of him anywhere. He's not at home; his car's not at work and I don't think he's been in an accident. I've checked all the major A&E units for 20 miles around. I've got this dreadful feeling... we need to find him. Fast.'

Copeland replied: 'I agree Inspector. We'll begin a search at first light. I'll get Essex police to put up their helicopter and take a look at Pilling's depot. I'll also alert them to the possibility of Wilson being held somewhere. And I'll move one of our tactical firearms units to Colchester, just in case.'

CHAPTER 22

Shrouded in the eternal blackness of the hood, Ray had no idea whether it was day or night or how many hours had passed since he heard people leaving. But he heard their return; heard them moving as silently as possible around the room, no words exchanged between them. He guessed there were three, possibly four of them.

Then he heard a plug being pushed into a socket, followed a few seconds later by a fizzing sound.

Were it not for the hood, he would have seen Mike Pilling holding a rheostat voltage controller, linked to a transformer plugged into the mains. The rheostat was connected to a bronze-tipped wand with an insulated handle, gripped expectantly and excitedly by George Curtis.

The device was a picana, a simple but effective instrument of torture that could deliver very high voltage, low current electric shocks, causing excruciating pain but with little or no soft tissue damage, especially when it was applied to sensitive parts of the body. It had been extremely popular amongst South American dictatorships in the 1970s.

It belonged to Adelina, who had used it ruthlessly in enforcing her will, especially on people she deemed to be her enemies, and had been packed by Gennaro who, knowing the purpose of their mission and his mistress's penchant for inflicting suffering, thought it would be a good idea.

Ray suddenly felt his boxer shorts ripped from him, leaving him completely naked. Then, he was doused in cold water. His body tensed in the expectation of pain but before anything else could happen, he heard a soft, gentle voice — which in different circumstances he might even have considered sexy — say: 'Let me do that.'

The tone of the voice hardened when its owner added: 'Get that hood off him. I want him to see my face.'

Ray blinked several times as his eyes became accustomed to the light; even though it wasn't brilliant it was many times brighter than the total darkness within the hood. He found himself staring into the two big pools of green that were Adelina's eyes. She held his gaze and waved the picana in front of him.

'I don't yet know who you are,' she said, 'but you will tell me. And you will also tell me who you work for and what you are doing here. You might be foolish enough to think you can resist me, but you can't. You will tell me everything I want to know because if you don't, this is what will happen.'

She gave a cursory nod to Gennaro who was now holding the rheostat.

Then she touched the tip of the picana to Ray's right nipple.

He stiffened and gritted his teeth as the pain of 6,000 volts surged through his body, the natural electrical resistance of his skin reduced by the water that had been thrown over him. He felt his muscles contract and his fists clench involuntarily as the power coursed around him.

After ten seconds she removed the wand and his body went limp.

'Now,' he heard her say, 'that was just a taste. If I have to use this again, the voltage will be higher and it will be applied for longer. Do you understand?'

Ray's response was: 'Fuck you.'

'I see we want to play the hard man. Very well. Let's start with something easy. What is your real name?'

'Welbourne. Raymond Welbourne.'

'Not good enough.' Turning to Gennaro she added: 'Turn it up to 7,000.'

Then she touched the picana to Ray's left testicle and held it there for twenty seconds. By the time she removed it perspiration covered his body, making his skin even more vulnerable to the next shock.

'And tell me Mr Welbourne, who do you work for?'

'Pilling Transport.'

'No you don't Mr Welbourne; not really. Tell me who your real employers are.'

'I've told you, Pilling Transport.'

'Double it,' she instructed Gennaro. This time the wand was applied to Ray's right testicle.

Those in the room saw him visibly shaking against the metal bed frame to which he was tied as 14,000 volts flowed through him. When it was over, his muscles were in spasm and his body danced the dance of extreme pain all by itself.

'One more time Mr Welbourne. Who are you and who do you work for?' Her voice had returned to its soft gentility. 'But before you answer me, let me tell you something about me because I think it might influence your answers.

'My name is Adelina Dalla Montagna but it has not always been so. I was born Elisabetta Barsotti but it was changed by my lover and soulmate, who decided I should have a name that was grander, more beautiful.

'My lover was someone who I believe was known to you. His name was Kamil Behar.'

At the very mention of the name of his nemesis, Ray stiffened, even through the residual pain. It was a movement that did not go unnoticed by Adelina but she chose to make no comment.

'Kamil had built up a business empire,' she went on, 'an empire that I know some people think is nothing more than a criminal enterprise but I prefer to think of it as a global network that supplies solutions to people's demands.

'And I also know that your police in Britain think Michael Pilling is the head of that organisation, but he isn't. I am. And I have been ever since you killed my Kamil.'

His brain numbed and confused by the electrical torture Ray spat: 'I didn't kill Behar, I was...'

Adelina allowed herself a wry smile. 'At last, we're getting somewhere,' she said.

'Now, let's start all over again. I think your real name is Wilson and that you are a policeman who is spying on us. That *is* the case, isn't it Mr Wilson?'

'Fuck you.'

'Add four,' Adelina said to Gennaro, holding the wand to Ray's penis and keeping it there.

Ray would never find adequate words to describe the agony of that electric shock. Every fibre of his body felt like it was on fire; he lost control of his bladder and urinated; his brain felt like it was trying to burst from his skull and he imagined his blood was boiling. The pain seemed to go on for hours. In fact it lasted less than 30 seconds.

When finally it was over, his body once more did the bizarre dance of the uncontrolled.

Adelina watched as the muscle twitching and spasms gradually subsided and for a brief moment considered turning the rheostat as high as it would go. But then she had second thoughts. She clicked her fingers at George Curtis and pointed at another implement that sat in a supermarket plastic bag on the floor. An electric drill.

'Mr Wilson, or Welbourne, or whatever your name is, I'm becoming bored with this game,' she said. 'I need answers and I need them now so I'm afraid I am going to have to stop treating you so gently.'

There was a high pitched whine as Curtis pressed the trigger on the drill, sending an 11mm titanium-tipped bit spinning at 3,000 rpm.

'If you don't answer my questions satisfactorily, Mr Curtis here will apply this drill to your left kneecap until it comes out of the other side. Believe me, you will be begging me to listen to you when that happens. But just in case it doesn't persuade you to tell me what I want to know, he will repeat it on your right knee. And if you continue to be uncooperative that will be followed by both your ankles and then both your elbows.

'I believe it's called a six pack and I don't have to describe to you just how badly crippled you will be at the end of it, assuming, that is, you survive the shock.

'So, let us begin again...'

***

Unheard and unseen in the darkness of night, the Essex police helicopter had hovered 1,000 feet over the Pilling Transport depot, minutely examining the site through image intensifiers and an infra-red camera. The camera had picked up heat sources from what appeared to be five people in the middle of a large shed. It had also picked up the heat produced by the electrical charge of the picana.

The news was flashed to Bernard Copeland, who by now was ensconced in the Gold Control suite at Essex police's Chelmsford headquarters. He rapidly absorbed the information and its implications then radioed the NCA's tactical firearms unit, which was waiting for orders less than quarter of a mile from Pilling's depot.

'Go, go, go,' he told the unit's commander. 'Use all available means to extract our man. His life is at risk.'

The 18 men, three sergeants and one inspector that made up the TFU were identically dressed in black fireproof overalls and balaclavas, "NATO" helmets, gas masks, bullet-proof vests, heavy boots with shin and knee guards and Kevlar gloves. Each of them carried a 9mm Heckler

& Koch MP5SFA2 carbine and a Glock 17 pistol. They travelled in two unmarked, dark blue Mercedes Sprinter vans.

As dawn began to tinge the horizon with a rich band of crimson and gold, the vans pulled silently into the Pilling Transport depot. The inspector quickly identified the shed pinpointed by the helicopter surveillance and using only hand signals moved his men towards it.

In single file they crouched, waiting for the lock to be broken so they could get into the building. It took around two minutes with a small pneumatic drill to cut the lock but once inside they could see the dim glow of light coming from the room where Ray was being held.

Using only hand signals once more, the inspector directed eight men to the office, where they crouched under the window, four to each side of the door. The man to the left of the door was carrying an Enforcer, the 32lb Big Key battering ram, as well as his carbine and side-arm.

Curtis was kneeling down, lining up the drill with Ray's left knee when the world turned violently upside down.

First of all, the Enforcer shattered the office window into a million fragments. A fraction of a second later a stun grenade was thrown into the room at the same moment that the Enforcer splintered the door. The grenade detonated with a blinding flash — so bright no one in the room could see anything for several seconds — and a bang so loud that as well as loss of hearing, it robbed all five people of their balance by disturbing the fluid within the inner ear's utricle and saccule canals.

Ray would remember distant voices shouting: 'Armed police, armed police' but nothing else.

Because the grenade had done its job so effectively, he didn't see the bulk that was George Curtis produce a pistol from his trouser band and try to aim it at him. He didn't hear the two double shots as two of the policemen opened fire with their carbines. Nor did he hear Adelina's screams as the top of Curtis's head disappeared and a huge dark red stain erupted from his chest as he fell dead at Mike Pilling's feet.

He would have a vague recollection of hands cutting him down and of a deep Welsh baritone voice telling him: 'You're alright now mate. You're alright. We've got you.'

He would remember nothing of the paramedics arriving or of the rush to hospital, the ambulance escorted by police cars front and rear. By the time the convoy arrived at the hospital, Ray was unconscious, partly from the torture he had endured and partly from the hangover of the stun grenade.

Doctors gave him a thorough examination but decided he had suffered no lasting injuries. He was sedated and put in a private side ward. He awoke, briefly, 12 hours later, to find Jan sitting at his bedside, anxiety oozing from every pore.

'Ray. How are you feeling?' she asked.

'Just dandy,' he managed before he fell once more into a deep sleep.

It would be another six hours until he opened his eyes again. Jan was still there.

By then Pilling, Adelina and Gennaro were in prison, having been remanded in custody charged with kidnap and assault of a police officer; small beer to what they would eventually be charged with but enough to keep them safely locked up, even though their respective solicitors had advised them to give "no comment" interviews.

The watchers at GCHG had also identified the owner of the mobile phone that had been used to tip off Adelina that her operation had been breached.

Brian Muswell had been the senior civil servant in the Attorney General's office for the past five years. A qualified barrister, he prided himself on knowing everything that went on in his department, largely because of the rapport he had with the AG himself. And it was the AG himself, believing he could be trusted, who had told Muswell of the NCA's request for telephone and e-mail intercepts on Mike Pilling.

Muswell's career had been impeccable until his proclivity for skinny young women dressed up as schoolgirls — more than once he had insisted to colleagues: 'The sweetest meat is nearest the bone' — had brought him to the Hydra's attention.

Now, to his shame and disgrace six policemen, four of them heavily armed, had turned up at his office and arrested him in full view of his subordinates.

Three days after the Hydra's heads were taken down in Colchester, Ray and Jan sat side-by-side in the office of Charles Barker, Director of Operations at the NCA. Seated on either side of him were Michael Wilpshire, Director of the Organised Crime Command and Bernard Copeland, Director of the Border Policing Command.

Barker began: 'Chief Inspector Wilson and Inspector Holroyd we need to conduct a thorough de-brief on the undercover operation you have so successfully completed. But I am well aware of the circumstances surrounding the operation's denouement so I propose we leave it for another day.

'However, I just wanted to add my thanks to those of Mr Copeland and Mr Wilpshire for the superbly professional way in which both of you have conducted yourselves in very difficult and trying circumstances. I'm sure you will delighted to hear that as a direct result of your work, police in Holland, Belgium, Germany, Italy and Turkey have been able to round-up close on 50 other people who were at the top of the organisation we called Hydra.

'We have every reason to believe the organisation is now broken and ineffective.

'You might also like to know that in the coming days, police forces throughout the UK will be arresting and questioning every one of the 620 surviving men identified from the images that you Mr Wilson discovered at Pilling Transport. Undoubtedly many of them will face criminal charges.

'All in all it has been a very, very successful exercise but, as I said, we do need a full de-brief. So I have taken the liberty of booking the pair of you into the same hotel you stayed at prior to this operation for a further three nights. We at the NCA will pick up the entire tab. You need pay for nothing. So, go and enjoy London, enjoy the sights, relax then report back here in three days time.'

Ray and Jan stared at each in astonishment. They were ready for the de-brief to begin immediately but now they were being offered a free three-day holiday.

'Thank you sir. Thank you very much indeed,' said Ray. 'It will do us both good to relax and return with refreshed brains. Thank you.'

Twenty minutes later the NCA Jaguar dropped the pair of them outside the hotel in the Aldwych and a liveried doorman carried their bags inside, where the receptionist greeted them like long-standing, much-favoured clients. After signing in, both of them were shown to rooms that faced each other across a corridor on the second floor.

'Time for a shower I think,' Ray said, 'then I'll see you in the bar in an hour.'

Exactly 60 minutes later, Jan walked into the bar to find Ray already there, perched on a bar stool, contemplating a large tumbler of whisky.

'It's the twenty-five year-old Talisker single malt,' he told her by way of explanation. 'And saying that Barker is paying, it's a large one. Now, what can I get you?'

'I think I'll have the same as last time,' she replied.

Ray thought for a second then asked the barman: 'Can I have one of your cocktails please? I believe it's called a One DOM.'

'Certainly sir. Coming up.'

'I'm impressed,' said Jan. 'I didn't think you'd remember.'

'There are some things that are impossible to forget,' he said.

They chose a small table discretely placed at the end of the bar that allowed a view of the whole room. They were on their second round of drinks when Ray glanced towards the entrance and froze.

An attractive woman in her mid to late 30s, dyed blonde hair expensively and fashionably cut, had just walked in and was surveying the room. She wore a bright red Bolero-style jacket with a black pencil-line skirt that ended just below her knees. It was, however, slashed to mid-thigh so that every movement exposed her long, slender leg. She spotted Ray and sashayed across the floor towards him, a smile growing ever more expansive.

It was Sally O'Dwyer, the NCA "minder" and the woman who had stood him up in this very hotel months before.

'Well, well, well,' she said, 'as I live and breathe, if it isn't Ray Wilson. How's the yacht broking business?'

'It's very good, thank you Sally. And how is risk management treating you?'

'Oh, you know. Up and down. Do you mind if I join you?'

Without waiting to be invited, she plonked herself down in a chair facing Jan and crossed her legs so that the slashed skirt fell open provocatively.

'You still on the Talisker Ray? I think I might have one too.'

As Ray made his way to the bar she asked Jan: 'I'm not disturbing anything am I? It's just that I haven't seen Ray for ages. I arranged to meet him last time we shared a drink but I couldn't make it. So I feel like we have some unfinished business.'

Jan was feeling somewhere between embarrassed and angry but managed to keep control of herself.

'No. Not at all. We're not together or anything. We're just work colleagues.'

'So, are you in the yacht broking business too?'

'Something like that, yeah.'

Ray returned and put the single malt down in front of the unexpected guest, along with a small crystal jug of cold water.

'Ah yes. The small splash. Changes the flavour for the better I seem to remember you saying. Well cheers.'

She raised her glass in salutation. Ray and Jan followed suit.

'I was just saying to your friend that I hoped I wasn't interrupting anything and explaining that you and I had met before in this very bar and that we have some unfinished business. It would be nice if we could find time to finish it tonight.'

'Yes, no doubt it would be enjoyable,' said Ray, unable to stop his eyes wandering to Sally's left thigh. 'Will you ladies excuse me for a moment please?'

He rose, leaving the two of them sitting in silence and went out to the reception desk.

'Can you please send a bottle of chilled pink champagne to room 271? With two glasses?' he asked the receptionist.

'Certainly sir. It will be there in five minutes.'

He walked back towards the bar and paused in the entrance, observing Jan and Sally sitting together like the strangers they were, neither paying any attention to the other.

He made his way through the throng at the bar but remained standing at the table.

'I've decided,' he began, 'that there is some unfinished business that cannot be allowed to hang any longer. I think it's something we've both wanted but for various reasons we haven't been able to do it. So, come on, let's go.'

He held out his right hand.

Both women stared at him, disbelief written large over both their faces.

Jan, to whom the hand had been offered, took it and stood up.

'Goodbye,' she said to Sally. 'It's been so nice to meet you.'

Printed in Great Britain
by Amazon